I0710623

YOU GIVE GOOD GAME

A RIVALS TO LOVERS CONTEMPORARY ROMANCE

PACIFIC VISTA RANCH

CLAIRE MARTI

CLAIRE MARTI

This one is for Josie

CHAPTER 1

Grace Steele clasped her hands together, willing her pulse to slow down because when she considered, really considered, what she'd agreed to do, she wanted to seize a parachute and jump out of the plane. No matter that it was the most lavish private jet she'd ever seen, complete with pearlescent white walls, buttery leather loveseats, and opulent midnight-blue carpeting.

What had she done? She'd sworn to avoid Hollywood forever but here she was, perched on a dove-gray seat supple enough to be made into an Italian leather jacket.

When the producer of Celebrity Charity Champions had called her personally--because hello, she hadn't had an agent or manager in close to a decade--she'd almost hung up without hearing him out. But the man had caught her at a vulnerable moment. Ahem, maybe even a desperate moment. Tomato-Tomahto.

When he'd tossed out the lure of one million dollars paid directly to the winner's charity of choice, he'd reeled her in, easy as you please. The prize was too tempting to resist, even if the concept of appearing on television again was about as appealing as cage diving with sharks.

Although, judging by the other nine contestants sharing the ginormous cabin, maybe she had landed in the shark tank after all. She stole another glance across the aisle, checking out the competition. She was sure the Ken Doll-looking guy downing mouthfuls of whiskey was in one of those famous 90s boy bands; the gorgeous brunette was Isabella, a veteran dating show star; and the striking Black woman was a supermodel. The others looked vaguely familiar, but she couldn't necessarily place them.

A pit formed in her belly--her introverted self was panicking. These days she spent most of her time at her animal rescue, Golden Years Pet Sanctuary, because unlike people, dogs and cats were trustworthy. Especially show business types.

The sexy ginger sitting across from her was an athlete she recognized from the Olympics several years back--maybe the Winter Games? The fine hairs on the back of her neck prickled and she looked up to find him studying her.

He flashed straight white teeth and reached out a strong hand--his moss green eyes gleaming with humor. "So it looks like we're in for an interesting few weeks. I'm Toby but my friends call me Fox."

She slid her palm against his cool one and a frisson of *something* sparked up her arm. "I'm Grace. So since you're my opponent, which one should I call you?"

"We can be friendly rivals, right?" His smile expanded into a wolfish grin and his fingers tightened around hers.

Yeah, he was a charmer, for sure. She released his grip, leaned back, and tapped a finger against her lips. "How about I call you Toby for now and we'll see how it goes?"

Now it clicked--Toby McAvoy, an X-Games star and an Olympic gold medalist in snowboarding. So, Winter

Olympian with a reputation for loving the snow bunnies. Yeah, he was trouble waiting to happen.

He lounged back in his seat and in red board shorts and a white T-shirt, his lean, wiry frame was sinewy muscled perfection. Colorful tattoos covered one arm. He wasn't classically handsome. His face was too lean, his chin too sharp, and his red hair stuck up in unruly tufts. But his mouth was beautiful, with chiseled defined lips.

Why did he have to be so hot? Because the last thing she needed was to hook up with one of the other contestants, she'd keep him at arm's distance. She gazed out the oversized window, which revealed only pristine blue sky and sparkling azure water, not a speck of land in sight.

No distractions needed, especially not with a cocky daredevil.

Not when she'd been scrambling to figure out how to find a major infusion of cash to keep her non-profit viable. Not when she had a list of abandoned senior cats and dogs living on borrowed time, desperate for a second chance. Not when her 3 million TikTok followers were clamoring for more happy endings for animals who deserved to live out their final chapter in peace.

And since some new show matching philanthropic billionaires with competitors looking to win money for their charity had offered her a spot, she would face her fears and give it her all. For the animals' sake, she would risk another disastrous public failure. So now here she was careening through the air to a mystery location with a dozen strangers.

Suddenly, the plane rocked dramatically, and screams erupted throughout the cabin. Grace pitched forward out of her seat directly into Toby's lap. She squealed and braced her hands against his hard hot chest, but she couldn't prevent landing on top of him. Her breath escaped in an unsteady whoosh and the air between them thickened.

He steadied her with one powerful arm around her waist. "Don't worry, I've got you. You okay?"

She exhaled a nervous laugh and looked up. Their mouths were mere inches apart, close enough to catch the hint of cinnamon on his breath. Heat blossomed low in her belly, and she inhaled a steadying breath, working to tamp down her completely illogical desire to kiss him. She scooted back to her own seat and fastened her seatbelt.

The captain's voice came over the loudspeaker. "Stay calm, everyone. We've got some unexpected turbulence and I'm going to navigate around it. Nothing to worry about but please make sure you are seated with your seatbelts securely fastened."

"Most airplane crash fatalities are from small planes. We're over water. We're all going to die," a Real Housewife of *somewhere* with about a million dollars of jewelry adorning her neck and fingers, cried and dropped her head between her knees.

Betsy, the showrunner, waved her arm. "Everyone, listen up. Don't worry, our pilot is awesome, and turbulence isn't uncommon around here. Please don't stress out, we're in excellent hands. Everything is going to be fine."

Talk about a reminder she had more important things to worry about than being attracted to Toby--like if they were going to crash. Now wasn't the time to panic.

Soothing frightened cats and dogs was her jam so maybe she could help the group on the plane. Although she'd always been shy, if she pretended she was in front of the cameras, her years of training helped her project her voice.

She cleared her throat. "The captain said we'll be fine. We all just need to stay calm. Just take a few deep breaths."

The plane veered to the right and dropped altitude. Like a lot of altitude. *Oh crap.* She swallowed a scream and dug her fingers into the armrests. They *better* be fine.

"She's right. Everyone just keep it together. Panic isn't going to help the pilot fly us to safety." Toby caught her gaze and smiled reassuringly.

The speaker crackled and the captain said, "We're landing now, so hold on because it might be bumpy."

With that proclamation, Grace's life flashed before her eyes. No way was her story complete yet. And she certainly wasn't ending it in a fiery explosion with a bunch of strangers.

Her three-legged cat Luna needed her. She still hadn't met the love of her life, she hadn't saved all the animals, and she was one month away from her thirtieth birthday.

Nope, they had to land safely––no acceptable alternative existed.

CHAPTER 2

Toby gritted his teeth and reminded himself of his pro-snowboarding days when he'd lived to catch air in the half-pipe and clamored to be dropped by a helicopter into the backcountry. If he hadn't died throwing himself down a mountain on a 155-centimeter piece of fiberglass, no way was he going down now. Not when he hadn't chosen the danger.

Most of the passengers were in varying states of distress, but the beautiful Ms. Grace Steele was cool and calm and collected. Her air of quiet strength stood out in stark contrast to the others freaking out and impressed the hell out of him.

When she'd boarded the plane ahead of him, he couldn't help admiring her toned legs, exquisite heart-shaped face, and wide crystal blue eyes. But she was one of nine people he had to beat to win the money for his non-profit, Alpine Adaptive Athlete Foundation.

Then she'd landed right in his lap, a tangle of long limbs, soft curves, and delicious floral scent. Tempting him to slide his hands up, clasp her jaw, and slant his mouth against her pretty pink lips. To see if she tasted as sweet as she looked. He should have kissed her because, hell, now who knew if they'd get the chance.

No flames were visible, and no smoke darkened the air, so hopefully they would be fine. Although the captain's voice sounded a little shaky and disembodied for his comfort. The show producers had admirably kept it together too, despite the situation.

After a couple nerve-wracking minutes, the wheels touched down. Despite some swerving, they skidded to a stop. After a moment, cheers and applause erupted in the cabin. He dropped his head back against the seat and offered up a silent thank you. They weren't going to die today.

Toby glanced at Grace, who hadn't uttered a word. Her face was impassive––he couldn't read her but apparently she handled drama well. Grace was strong under pressure, which meant she could be a fierce contestant.

Another quality in the plus column and one more reason he needed to play it cool around her. No matter how every muscle in his body had leaped to attention when she'd tumbled into his lap, she was just one more rival––not a potential hook-up.

Toby rubbed the scruff on his jaw, glanced out the window, and contemplated the smooth pavement, yellow lines, and orange cones. Over the course of his career, he'd flown all over the world and it sure looked like they were on a traditional runway. Not in the middle of a random field or dangerous jungle or anything.

"Okay everyone, we're here. The camera crew is on the ground and will be filming us deplaning. I've got mics for all of you, which you'll wear at all times, except for in your private suites. And never fear, your reputations are still pristine because we didn't catch any of you crying or puking on film." Betsy smirked.

Seriously? Was she fucking kidding with this? Joking about the plane crashing?

Muttered protests filled the cabin. When he glanced at Grace, she was shaking her head, her lips pressed together in a tight line. Yeah, he wasn't the only one irritated with the flippant comment.

"Gather your things and line up for your wireless microphones. It's showtime."

After everyone had hooked on the small mics, one of the crew opened the plane door. A gust of crisp ocean breeze flowed inside. When he reached the doorway, the glare of the sun blasted into him like when he'd slammed into hard-packed snow during a wipe-out. He shaded his eyes from the brightness and descended the steps onto the tarmac.

Enormous palm trees, tall fir-green cypresses, and lush red flowers encircled the runway but didn't offer much in the way of shade. Yeah, his pale freckled skin would need industrial- strength sunscreen if he was going to survive outdoors.

His eyes adjusted to the glare enough to take in a long, single-story hangar with five open-sided Jeeps beside it. Several camera operators captured their arrival but otherwise, only nature surrounded them. They could be anywhere from the South Pacific to the Aegean Sea.

But the location didn't matter. What mattered was him stepping back into champion mode because he hadn't agreed to do a reality show for any other reason than winning the money. Although his Development Director was working on grants for his foundation, the charitable grant process was a logistical mire of red tape and held no guarantee of receiving funds. His friend Josh and all the other adaptive skiers and snowboarders depended on him so here he was, ready to roll.

"Listen up, your names are on your assigned vehicle. It's about a twenty minute drive to the estate. At 6 p.m., you'll meet your benefactor for our group dinner, and you'll learn what the competition will entail. Follow me." Betsy glanced around the group before turning and heading toward the hangar.

Toby sauntered toward the waiting fleet with everyone else. Back when he'd been a pro snowboarder, he'd reached the pinnacle partially by studying his challengers and learning their strengths and weaknesses. Tonight he'd continue observing his rivals and see what else they would reveal through their behavior and file every detail away.

Because understanding who he was up against helped him make decisions. Just like he'd do here.

And win.

CHAPTER 3

Grace spun in a circle and lifted her face toward the sky, savoring the sun's warm kiss on her skin. Her nerves were running high, especially after the long flight and the stressful landing.

"Chop-chop, Grace," Betsy called, "you're in Jeep Number Four with Toby and me. Let's go."

Her breath caught in her throat and her fingers curled around her purse strap. Figures she'd be paired up with the first guy who'd sparked her interest in over a year, especially after feeling his muscular arms wrapped around her and smelling his tart clean scent. At least the Jeeps were open-air.

Sun glinted off the camera lenses positioned around the landing strip. Time to employ her dormant acting skills––all those years starring on a popular sitcom hadn't gone to waste, right? She pasted on a smile, crossed the tarmac, and climbed into the utilitarian truck next to Toby. She immediately fastened her seatbelt––no more accidental launching into his arms.

"We meet again." Toby's lips twitched. With his cheeky

smile and magnetism, the guy was a total flirt. And probably used to women falling all over him.

Or maybe he was playing a role for the show? Turning on the charm and acting like Mr. Happy-Go-Lucky when in reality he was a fierce Olympic competitor.

She forced her shoulders to soften. She could play it cool. "I think we're all going to be spending a lot of time together."

Betsy peeled out, speeding down a tree-lined gravel lane. Balmy perfumed air brushed along her skin and Grace shifted her attention to the breathtaking scenery. They settled into a companionable silence

The Jeep hit a pothole, rocking the vehicle, and Grace bounced up in her seat, her feet lifting off the floor. She seized the safety pole to her left with both hands, managing to avoid grabbing Toby again.

"Sorry, guys. That was the roughest patch. The ride should be smooth from here on out." Betsy called over her shoulder. "Almost there."

Toby glanced at her death grip on the rail and chuckled. "Don't worry, Grace, I don't bite. I mean, not unless you ask nicely."

Annoyance flared down her spine. "Seriously? Look, I'm not trying to be rude but I'm here to save my animal rescue. So maybe dial it back a little bit?"

He held up both hands. "Got it, loud and clear. Just being friendly. I hate to burst your bubble but, I'm going to win for my disabled athletes' foundation."

She took a few cleansing breaths. At a young age, she'd learned that even the friendliest people looked out for themselves first. Allowing any of the other contestants too close was not an option, especially Foxy Toby. Of course he seemed nice and had an admirable cause, but she couldn't trust anyone. Because being one of the most famous child actors in the U.S., then losing it all thanks to her former actress "best friend's" betrayal and her manager mother's actions taught her an important lesson––never trust anyone in the entertainment industry.

She'd sworn to stay out of the public eye and after college, followed her dream to help senior animals. Somehow, being on camera again making TikToks with her cat Luna didn't feel like she was courting fame. Probably because her three-legged black cat was the focal point, not her.

Although the rumbling of the truck prohibited further conversation, she couldn't ignore her awareness of Toby. Like her, he was studying the landscape as they sped toward their destination, so she snuck a peek at his angular profile.

Yep, he was too cute, and his proximity was distracting. She returned her attention to the countryside. If she could have a few hours to herself, she could regain her composure. Or at least smell a little less ripe.

The tree-shrouded lane opened into a wide clearing framed by soaring Cypresses. In the distance, a sprawling white building appeared above the rolling terrain. Grace pressed one hand to her throat. "Wow."

Betsy barked out a laugh. "Wait until you see the rest of the estate. Your minds will officially be blown."

The other Jeeps rolled in and within a few short minutes, they were piling out of the vehicles. More production assistants waited, and a few camera people recorded them from around a large pergola-covered patio dotted with low-slung couches and tables, framed with fuchsia bougainvillea.

A hint of salty breeze wafted through the air, cooling the damp strands on the back of Grace's neck. Between the open Jeep and sitting next to Toby––something she'd be careful to avoid––she was a sweaty mess.

"Please take your envelope and follow the path to the right of me. Your private bungalow's name is inside, along with some other basic information. You can take off your mics in your suites but please wear them to dinner," Alanna, a petite brown woman with tight-black curls, announced and held up a stack of cream-colored packets.

"FYI––we don't have locks on the bungalows. The island is secure and privately owned. See you all in the courtyard at 6 p.m. sharp. Tonight we'll also be starting with the interview booth so don't be surprised when you get a tap on your shoulder."

Grace accepted her envelope, grabbed her suitcase's handle, and proceeded toward her room along the wide slate-paved pathway lined with fragrant shrubs and trees. When she reached the single-story white-washed bungalow, she paused at the door and admired the wide windows and turquoise shutters. A noise behind her had her turning.

And, of course, there stood Toby in front of the bungalow directly across from hers. The afternoon light bounced off the lens of the wall-mounted camera above his door. Someone was always watching.

Toby flashed a quick grin and waved a hand. "Hey neighbor. Want to check out the grounds and walk down to the courtyard together?"

Grace stiffened but forced her lips to curve upward. No need for the producers to see she was anything other than cordial. "Hey Toby. Oh, thanks, but don't wait for me. I need a shower, so I'll see you at dinner."

His deep green eyes widened, and she kicked herself internally––yeah, way to reference getting naked.

She hurried inside, slammed the ornately carved teak door behind her, and leaned her head back against the smooth wood. Time to cool off, in every sense of the word. And time to remember that every moment outside of her room, she would be on film. Was Toby being flirtatious just for the cameras despite her earlier brush-off?

She yanked off her microphone and tossed it on the small table next to the entrance.

Part of her strategy for this entire competition was to keep the others at arm's length. But no way would she be cast as the resident villain by the producers, so she'd have to be mindful of not coming across as too aloof. Winning this competition was the difference between saving hundreds more senior animals and…well, not. Life or death.

She dragged her luggage into the spacious high-ceilinged suite, tossed it onto the baggage rack, and pulled out her toiletry bag. Plenty of time to admire the King-sized bed with its teak bed frame and the luxurious furnishings later. When she reached the enormous bathroom that resembled something out of a home decorating show, she almost cried with joy when she saw the double-headed rain shower.

Time to clean her body, clear her mind, and get focused on why she was here. The animals.

CHAPTER 4

An old-school gong sounded close by, and Toby picked up his pace. A gull squawked overhead, and hints of salt filled the air so, although he couldn't see the sea, it had to be close. His only company on the walkway was a small lizard that skittered past him into the dense shrubs. He reached an enormous courtyard and sucked in a steadying breath.

The beauty of the place blasted into him. Twisting vines of red bougainvillea spread haphazardly up the white-washed walls of the two-story building to the slanting charcoal-tiled roof. Olive trees woven with sparkling lights sat in large ceramic pots around the perimeter. Tables covered with turquoise tablecloths were set up around the courtyard, with sparkling crystal, white plates, and seats with place cards.

He crossed the space and, because he was apparently being punished for some past sins, he was seated next to Grace. Or maybe the producers kept throwing them together for a reason? During the casting interviews, they'd asked a lot of questions about his past relationships, and he'd admitted his two former serious girlfriends had cheated on him. Just like his dad had been unfaithful to his mom. But he'd acted casual, like he didn't care.

Another gust of wind lifted the edges of Grace's long, shiny hair and brought its sweet floral scent to his nose. Damn, she smelled like heaven. And he'd probably never forget the feel of her curves and silky skin when she'd landed in his lap. Or the vision of her slick and slippery in the shower, just across the path from him. When he pulled out his chair, she looked up and flashed a Mona Lisa smile.

Yeah, Grace was a mystery, like the enigmatic model in the famous painting. And she had made it crystal fucking clear she wasn't into him. He'd heard a couple of the other contestants gossiping about her starring in *Molly's World* and some scandal when she'd left Hollywood for good. Maybe she was doing this show in part to revive her acting career? Color him intrigued—despite her earlier rebuff, he wanted to know more about her.

Yeah, he was here to save his charity, but she was already a major distraction, so what harm would a little flirtation do? The sparks between them weren't his imagination. He was the king of no-strings and banter, and a few kisses wouldn't deter from the end game. If the producers kept seating them together, he had to make the best of it, right?

Betsy's voice streamed through the tall speakers positioned next to a low dais. "Good evening everyone, now it's time to meet your host. Not only is she the creator of some of the most iconic perfumes in the world, but she's also one of the biggest philanthropists in the world, donating millions each year to worthy causes.

"Usually, she shuns the spotlight, but we are fortunate to have her host the inaugural Celebrity Charity Champions where she will donate one million dollars to one of your non-profit organizations. Please put your hands together for Frances Ellis."

Applause filled the vast courtyard and a tiny platinum blonde wearing a flowing white dress strode on to the stage. She flashed a brilliant smile, surveying the group with a nod of her head, and in a polished British accent said, "Thank you all for being here. I'm thrilled to be your host and I'm pleased you all arrived at my home safely."

Toby's jaw dropped--this castle or manor or whatever the hell it was--was her home? Wow. Next to him, Grace gasped.

"Tonight, we'll be dining together underneath the stars. Tomorrow, you'll have time to explore the beaches and hills of my island and adjust to the time change. I know you've traveled a long way, and the competition will be fierce so you'll have the day to reset and rejuvenate because afterward, every moment will be devoted to the contest.

Grace turned to him, her arctic blue eyes wide. "Her island?" She mouthed the words.

Maybe Grace wasn't going to freeze him out completely after all.

For once in his life, he didn't have a quick reply, so he shrugged a shoulder.

"We are in the Ionian Sea on the island of Diosa. The closest island with which you may be familiar is Corfu. This palazzo and the surrounding property have been in my grandmother's family for over three-hundred years."

She held up one finger. "In a nod to my maternal grandfather, Round One of the competition is inspired by the Scottish Highland Games. The events will require speed, agility, and strategy."

The slick looking Ken Doll's brows drew together, the Big Bad Bald Dude smirked, and the plastic-looking brunette looked like she was sucking on a lemon. Probably worried about breaking a nail or dropping a hair extension.

Grace shifted and crossed one long leg over the other, exposing a mouthwatering glimpse of tanned thigh and muttered something under her breath that sounded distinctly like, "Oh fuck."

He glanced at her, and her teeth were worrying her full lower lip, which was painted a distracting glossy pink. He adjusted in his chair, his pants suddenly too tight.

"I will fill you in on the second and third rounds as we progress. But, before we're served, let's introduce our contestants."

Toby picked up his wineglass and downed a mouthful of crisp white wine and snuck a cursory glance at the others at the table––time to pay attention and learn more about his rivals.

Frances pointed to a tall, slender Black woman wearing a fuchsia jumpsuit. "At the first table, we have Karina, who you all may recognize as one of the top supermodels in the world. Next to her, sits Isabella, from The Bachelor franchise."

Frances continued, "I'm sure we've all danced to some of Joey's songs when he was in everyone's favorite 90s boy band."

All eyes turned toward Ken Doll––aka Joey––who still sported the boy band hair. The guy was gym-fit, but he'd sipped whiskey all day on the plane so if he was hungover or buzzed all the time, those muscles wouldn't get him far.

"Melissa is in the gorgeous emerald blouse and she's one of the most renowned Michelin star chefs in the world."

The curvy middle-aged woman swept one hand along her front. "I think you know I'm a chef and feats of strength for me are more beating a stiff meringue and less tossing a shot-put. Just how athletic is this first round? Will someone like me have a chance against, say, someone like him?" She pointed to the bald guy.

"Yes, Melissa, I'm aware of your culinary reputation. And of course, when we selected each one of you to be here, we worked to keep the playing field fair. Now everyone hold your questions until I've finished please."

"As for Clayton, yes he's a former football player and likely physically strongest, but each one of you has special skills that will serve you throughout the games. Remember, Round One is just part of the whole."

The guy rolled his massive shoulders and flared his nostrils. Kind of like a massive bull about to charge. "I prefer Clay." His voice was soft and slightly menacing.

Yeah, Toby would remember never to address Clay by his full name or hell, ever look him in the eye.

"At the second table, we have Weston, the action movie star seated next to Isaac, who was also on The Bachelor franchise." The Mario Lopez-looking guy must be Isaac, judging by the smirk he directed at Isabella.

Frances held up one hand. "Just a few more. Kimmelle is one of the most beloved Real Housewives of that franchise. Finally, we have Grace, an adored child star seated next to Toby, our Olympic snowboarding champion. You all bring unique gifts to this experience, but you are all philanthropists, so you have that generosity of spirit in common, no matter if your strengths are more physical, mental, or emotional."

Frances's scarlet lips curved upward. "Now let's enjoy your first meal on Diosa." She joined the producers at the table on the far end of the courtyard.

Grace placed one hand over her mouth and whispered to him, "Okay, this is getting interesting."

Like him, Grace was also an observer and gathering intel on the competition.

He turned toward Grace and quirked a brow. "Did you get all that?"

A smile danced on her lips. "Absolutely not. But let the games begin."

Her quiet composure intrigued him--what lay beneath the surface of her seemingly placid exterior? Was she acting or was she shy? Still waters run deep and all that. Of course he wanted to dive deeper and unravel her secrets.

But every single person here was an obstacle in the way of him fulfilling his promises to his best friend Josh, who he'd started his foundation for, and all the disabled athletes who thrived in the community he'd created. He'd have to keep reminding himself of the end goal and maintain his distance.

No matter how attracted he was to the beautiful, mysterious Grace.

CHAPTER 5

*J*nterview Booth: Evening #1

GRACE SHIFTED on the hard wooden chair that may have been on the island since Frances's ancestors built the palazzo. More Inquisition than modern luxury. The room was the size of a closet and just as dark--not claustrophobic at all. Ha.

A light flicked on, and a disembodied voice spoke from a speaker mounted on the opposite wall. Aha, the camera was behind the screen. Show time.

"Welcome to Diosa, Grace. We're excited to have you on Celebrity Charity Champions. Can you share with our viewers a little about why they should root for you and your charity?"

She smiled for the camera. "Thanks, I'm excited to be here. Well, back when I was a kid, I found a cute dog tied up to a tree with a note on her collar that said, "Free to a good home." Long story short, she'd been abandoned because she was twelve years old, the same age as I was, and had medical issues. We adopted her and Sunny became my best friend. I founded Golden Years Pet Sanctuary six years ago in her honor."

"That's a sweet story. So your sanctuary is for senior animals?"

She nodded, "Yes. My animal rescue focuses on matching abandoned senior cats and dogs with people who want to spoil them rotten." Warmth spread through her because she'd succeeded in making a difference.

"I think our audience will definitely be rooting for you, Grace. Now tell us, who do you think your biggest rival will be? Who is the person to beat?"

Her pulse kicked up––the producers diving right into creating some drama. She shrugged a shoulder. "We've just arrived and I'm sure everyone here is a worthy rival."

"Surely you have some idea? Come on, give us your first impressions."

Not a chance in hell. She held up her hands. "I don't like to make snap judgments, so I really think we've all got a shot at the money."

"Grace Steele, playing it close to the vest. Well, good luck out there. We'll look forward to hearing how it goes." The camera clicked off.

She'd survived interview number one. At least they hadn't asked about Toby.

TOBY SCANNED THE DIM ROOM, waiting for someone to come in or something to happen. The jet lag was catching up with him and if they left him in the dark, he'd pass out in the next couple of minutes.

His eyelids were growing heavy when a monotone voice spoke from a speaker somewhere across from him.

"Welcome, Toby. We're huge snowboarding fans and we know our audience is, too. You're an Olympic gold medalist. Do you think you're the one to beat?"

So yeah, he'd be talking to a camera hidden in a black wall. Totally natural. But he knew how to handle the press, and this was no different. He grinned. "Absolutely. I'm here to finish first."

"Love the confidence. Can you share a little about your charity with the audience?"

"Definitely. Alpine Adaptive Athlete Foundation works with disabled athletes to get them back on the slopes. We do everything from education to training to providing special equipment." And the smiles on people's faces were worth every minute.

"That's incredible. And it was a huge deal when you walked away from your successful career to start the foundation, right?"

His jaw tightened but he kept his expression loose. "I don't know about that."

"Well, we missed seeing you in the half-pipe. Do you miss competing?"

Irritation flared through him. "I'm here to compete now, right? And for a good cause."

"Fair point. Well, good luck Toby. We know you're going to be one to watch."

And with that parting line, they were done. Time to crash and make sure he lived up to expectations––his and the audiences'.

CHAPTER 6

"*Y*ou've got to be kidding me," Grace blew out a breath once she reached the huge grass field and realized just what Round One of the Games would entail.

Because when she saw the 7-foot beast with legs like oak trees sporting a kilt and carrying what appeared to be an actual tree trunk, her belly lurched, and she froze. Because she'd been an avid *Outlander* viewer--for the history lessons and not to ogle Jamie--she'd ended up diving down the rabbit hole of Scottish festivals and Highland Games.

"C'mon over." The enormous creature waved an arm the size of a ham hock.

A hand tapped her shoulder and there was Toby, his sensual mouth curved into a playful grin. Sparks danced along her skin, and she stepped away from him. Time to retreat.

The rest of the group had also arrived. Had she lost a moment in the sheer horror of what was to come? Yeah, her faculties were sharp, sharp, sharp. And apparently, her demise was barreling toward her in the form of a twenty-foot log.

They traipsed across the crisp grass to meet their fates. Of course, the camera crew was set up around the perimeter of the field, eager to immortalize the fun. Or humiliation, depending on whose turn it was.

"Morning everyone. I'm Douglas and I'll be running this portion of today's competition. I'm from Inverness and I'm a professional Highland Games competitor. We'll be having three individual events––the hammer throw, the caber toss, and archery. We've swapped out the shotput for archery to give some of the..." He cleared his throat. "Less athletic competitors a chance. Then, you'll be in two teams for the tug-o-war this afternoon."

Isabella, clad in a minuscule neon yellow sports bra and booty shorts, tossed her high ponytail over one sculpted shoulder. "Please tell me you're going to teach us and let us practice this before we actually compete?"

"Aye. Now come a little closer and I'll show you the hammer throw." He barked out a laugh.

Grace's stomach churned. Because after this experience, she'd need to fill her private pool with ice and submerge up to her forehead. For hours. Maybe overnight.

Unless she beamed someone in the head with one of the large dangerous objects and was disqualified. How the hell was she supposed to lift a 150-lb log? At least that's what she'd heard the logs for the caber toss weighed. Her shoulders ached already. She wasn't going to allow the panic curling up her spine to derail her though. *Think of Luna. Think of all the animals who need you. Suck it up.*

Toby leaned in and whispered, "Piece of cake." His voice was raspy. Sexy. And caused goosebumps to pop up along her skin.

How was he so close to her again? She gave him side-eye. "Sure, because that log is about the same size you are."

Toby the Fox was also a smart-ass, which was her personal brand of catnip, and of course made him more attractive. Nobody in their right mind would find these games easy. He might be able to fly down a snow-packed mountain, but he wasn't in his element anymore. Not that she was either, but still.

The group inched forward as Douglas picked up an iron ball that appeared to be on the end of a chain. "I'll demo it a few times and then you'll take turns." With that pronouncement, he spun in three circles and flung the ball. It whirred through the air before landing with a metallic thud.

Grace gasped before clapping along with everyone else. Holy crap, the guy's unexpected grace and agility were impressive. Like an elephant performing a perfect pirouette. Without another word, he repeated the process and the ball landed beyond the initial one.

He turned and lifted his meaty arms. "There we go. It's a breeze. Who's going first?"

In a move that surprised absolutely nobody, judging by the murmurs, Clay swaggered like a peacock toward Douglas. He wore a black muscle tank and basketball shorts, showcasing his burly physique. But next to the Scotsman, he wasn't the giant any longer.

While Douglas gave Clay a few pointers, Grace turned to Toby with raised brows. "Still a piece of cake?"

"You'll be surprised because this one is easier than it looks. A lot of non-Goliaths can throw a respectable distance. It's only about twenty pounds so just put your whole body into it and use momentum."

"You're an expert on Highland Games? Seriously?" And why was he being so helpful? Was he genuine or was he acting for the cameras?

He grinned, a hint of dimple appearing in one lean cheek. "Hey, I come by this hair and these freckles honestly. I've been to Scotland before and attended a few festivals. And not all the players are built like those two."

"Aren't you my bitter rival? Why are you giving me tips?" They were competing to win. Was he trying to get her to lower her guard?

"Like I said, Scotland's in me blood. I'm the favorite to win, wee lassie," he declared with a godawful brogue.

She snorted and fired back with her own perfect brogue. "Wee lassie. Good one. And if this was scripted television, you'd be fired on the spot for your pathetic accent, laddie."

He stumbled back a step and pressed a hand to his heart. "You've been hiding your pure Scottish blood from me. How can this be?"

"Hey, lovebirds, you two are up next so pay attention." Douglas's heavy brow furrowed.

Oops, not good to catch the instructor's eye, especially when heavy equipment was involved. Nor to be pegged as "lovebirds" on camera and have the producers edit the entire show with that filter.

"No Scottish blood, I'm just great at accents." With that parting shot, she moved to the other side of the group. Safer that way.

Time to separate herself from Toby--it was too easy to hang out with him and her focus needed to be one thousand percent on the competition.

Then, Toby sauntered up and easy as you please, threw the damn hammer further than Clay on his first try. Of course he did.

Douglas roared his approval and held up Toby's arm. "Now this is proof that you don't have to be a big strappin' man to do this. Bravo little fellow."

Laughs and snorts erupted, but Toby didn't flinch as he strutted back to the group. "A win's a win."

"Now you, in the robin's egg blue, your boy here set the example. You're up. Don't be scared––it's about the weight of your pocketbook, aye?" He guffawed again.

Grace's shoulders stiffened. *Her pocketbook?* She'd show this big Neanderthal she wasn't afraid. She marched across the springy grass and without a word picked up one of the balls or hammers or whatever the dumb things were called. It weighed about the same as one of the kitty litter containers she lugged around all the time.

Although she only poured litter into litterboxes and didn't toss it across fields. But she could do this. Squeezing her eyes shut, she pivoted into a turn and swung the contraption around, one, two, three times, before throwing it with as much force as possible. When she opened them, searched the field for it before looking down.

And it was about two feet from where she stood. Nowhere near the distance it needed to travel. A few snickers erupted from the group behind her, but she refused to acknowledge it.

To his credit, Douglas didn't laugh outright but his face had a suspicious crimson hue when he walked over, collected all three of the hammers, and carried them back in one over-sized paw. "You used your arms too much and didn't put your full weight into it. You're not a petite lass, so this time, plant your foot, use your center of gravity and less wrist."

Grace gritted her teeth. And yes, she was aware she wasn't "petite"––part of the reason she'd outgrown her childhood acting career. Like it was her fault she wasn't built like the ballerina she'd played on *Molly's World* until she hit puberty. Boobs and hips were normal, right? Not according to Hollywood.

Persistence was one of her strengths and she'd do better.

This time, she channeled her frustration and focused on the technique. The iron ball landed about a foot beyond her prior attempt, but no way was she winning this event. Not even close.

Douglas grunted and waved his arm. "Better. Okay, who's next. Let's get this practice moving."

"So maybe I'm not moving to Scotland." Grace returned to the group, forcing her poker face to remain in place.

Part of dealing with rivals was never allowing them to see if something bothered you. The other nine people all wanted to win just as much as she did. Toby had made his position clear, anyway.

Toby winked at her. "Great effort, lassie." His brogue remained atrocious, but she appreciated his positivity.

"You did great. And there are other events, thank the goddess, because the odds of me succeeding at this one or carrying a tree bigger than I am are like the odds of Margot Robbie asking me to marry her." Melissa, the chef, flashed a warm smile.

"Thanks, Melissa. Margot would be lucky to be your wife. Let's hope you're right on the other events." Although her only hope was the archery because the log wasn't happening.

The camera crew filmed every moment and yeah, Grace was certain she'd love the shots of her looking slow, sweaty, and sad. The bigger guys and Kimmelle both killed the caber toss and how they all carried a twenty foot, 150-pound log in two hands was a mystery. So finishing dead frickin' last in both events wasn't exactly a shocker.

But the disappointment was real. And if the competition was all sports, unless they were swimming or playing pickleball, she didn't stand a chance. Sure she was fit, but more than one person had commented on the irony of Grace being her first name, because it definitely wasn't her middle one.

Toby was the best--graceful and powerful in his wiry

strength. He made both the hammer throw and the caber toss look like...a piece of cake. Once an Olympian and all that. He'd set the bar for the rest of the competition as the one to beat. And damn if the sweat gleaming on his sinewy muscles didn't make him look even sexier.

Surprisingly, when they trooped back to the target area, Toby choked and none of his arrows hit the bullseye. His jaw tightened and his eyes narrowed, no evidence of his customary easygoing grin.

For the first time, Grace caught a glimpse of his competitive streak. Not so laidback when he didn't finish first. She'd file that information away in the vault to contemplate later.

When she stepped up for her turn, much to her shock, all three of her arrows hit dead center and she won the event. Apparently, she could channel the Goddess Artemis with a bow and arrow. Go figure. Hell yes, she'd take the gold medal in archery

Heading into the afternoon, she and Toby were in the lead. All the more reason to maintain her distance. If she succumbed to his charming flirtation, she'd give him the upper hand. And give the producers a showmance to exploit. No way.

This morning was only one part of the competition and she'd keep her focus on the next event.

CHAPTER 7

Toby's assigned position at the back of the tug-o-war line was--shocker--directly behind Grace. Like having her perfectly rounded, athletic curves against him while they tugged the thick rope together wouldn't mess with his concentration.

They'd relocated to a different grassy expanse, which had been hidden by a hedge of Cypress trees. And yeah, there was a giant mud pit that some or all of them would be landing in later. Grace was sandwiched between him and Joey, with Isabella and Weston completing their team. Clay was the anchor for the other team and his bulk would be a decided advantage.

He glanced down and massaged the back of his neck. Time to get Grace off the brain because the woman was occupying too much of his headspace. Banter and flirting were as natural as breathing to him and didn't usually affect him but being around Grace felt like…more.

His head jerked up at the shrill whistle.

Frances Ellis, wearing a black and white striped referee jersey and black athletic pants, called out, "Hello warriors. I'll be at the center line judging the tug-o-war. You'll be assessed based on your teamwork and, of course, on who wins the pull. This will be best two out of three. Are you ready?"

Everyone yelled their assent.

She gave a sharp nod. "I do love this event, it's bloody good fun. Now pick up the rope. We'll go on the count of three."

Grace bent over at the same time he did, and his face came dangerously close to her peach-shaped ass. He grabbed the rope and stood quickly––he was in trouble. Because instinct had him opening his mouth to take a bite. And his instincts were obviously not his friend. Grace was hot as hell but all this proximity, especially now she was sweaty and flushed, was killing him.

Tug-o-war. Win the team contest. Focus dude.

He glanced at Grace's firm grip around the rope and was instantly hard. *Don't visualize those long fingers wrapped around my dick.*

He cleared his throat. "Make sure to keep a slight bend in your knees and dig in your heels. We're gonna win this one."

She angled her head back and gave a small nod, determination gleaming in her narrowed eyes. "Damn right we are."

"Competitors, pull in three, two, one!" Frances shouted.

A dramatic tug dragged them forward and Toby stumbled into Grace's back before he could catch himself. The terrain was sandy and slippery, and he needed to get grounded. He shifted his weight back into a shallow squat and tightened his grip, the rope's rough fibers burning his palms. Grunts and shouts filled the air. Sweat trickled down his brow.

They managed to hold the line and shifted a minuscule distance back. Grace's ponytail hit his chest, the silky strands teasing his skin and he swallowed a groan. She leaned back, the muscles in her sculpted arms straining with effort.

Perspiration glistened slick on her golden skin. He blew out a breath and pulled harder.

Another yank lurched the entire team forward sending Joey and Isabella stumbling into the water. A whistle blew. They'd lost. *Shit.*

"Round One goes to Team A. You've got a three minute break to regroup."

Damn it. His usual laser focus had been scattered because of Grace. They had to win this event which meant he needed to get away from her. As far away from her as possible because obviously he'd lost his mind.

Toby dropped the rope and called to Frances. "Can we change positions? Let me be up front and have Weston be the anchor?"

"Go ahead. Do what you think it takes to win." Frances waved one hand.

The actor's shorts and tank top were drenched, and his jaw was set––yeah, Weston wouldn't argue about moving away from the mud puddle.

The team huddled together. "Sorry guys, I take responsibility for that one. Let's swap." Damn it, he needed distance from Grace and her perfect ass.

Isabella shrugged. "I agree with Toby. Weston's got twenty pounds on him and would be a better anchor. I don't fancy going into that disgusting pond again, either. Why don't you and Grace move up front and we'll take the anchor spots."

Toby's nostrils flared. "I'll swap but Grace should stay where she is. She'll do better in the back, and we've got to beat them."

Grace hissed out a breath, crossed her arms across her chest, and gave him side-eye. Shit, now she probably assumed he thought she was the weak link when in fact, it was him. But nothing to do about it now.

Grace shrugged. "I'm fine with wherever you guys want me." The ice in her arctic blue eyes belied her casual tone.

He marched to the front of the line––he had to focus on the competition and his own sanity because she was driving him wild. There was something about the woman that made him yearn for something more.

"Make sure to dig your heels in this time, Toby," Grace called in a snarky tone, mirroring his earlier advice.

He rolled his eyes behind his mirrored aviators and assumed his new position. Better to brave the death glare of the other team than get lost in Grace's beauty. He signed up for this show to save his beloved foundation, not to repeat his pattern of falling for unavailable women.

When Frances called Round Two, Toby kept his eye on the prize and apparently Weston did a better job holding up the rear. Without too much struggle, they sent Clay's team tumbling into the water amidst curses and screams.

Now, they were tied. The final round of tug-o-war would determine today's winner. And he needed those points to build upon his lead. Because who knew what the remainder of the competition would be? His athleticism was his greatest strength so, today could be his best chance to secure a victory.

After a quick huddle, they agreed to repeat their strategy. Of course, Grace looked even sexier now that her tissue-thin pale blue tank top was soaked with sweat. A gust of ocean breeze cooled his skin and when it reached her and her nipples peaked, his self-control almost snapped. Damn, what he wouldn't give to sweep her up in his arms and drag her off somewhere private.

Her eyes lifted and a flicker of awareness hummed between them. She moistened her upper lip and retreated a step. Every muscle in his body stiffened. *Damn.*

He shook his head, gazed around their small circle, and clapped his hands. "Let's do this. We've got them."

This time, it wasn't so easy. They stumbled a few steps forward, almost to the neon yellow dividing line. Then, they burrowed in and inched back. Toby gritted his teeth and honed his focus on the present moment, like he used to on the mountain. Everything faded away except for the coarseness of the rope, the strain of his muscles, and the competitors' shouts.

"We've got them. Finish it now," Grace shouted, and her voice goaded him to push harder.

And then Frances blew the whistle and declared Team B the winners. They hadn't tossed Clay's team into the mud, but they'd forced them across the line, which was enough. Clay's black eyes glowed like embers from hell. Man, the dude was scary.

Isabella and Weston were holding hands jumping up and down. Grace wouldn't look at him but caught one of his hands and one of Joey's and they were dancing around, singing "We Are The Champions" at the top of their lungs.

The joy of victory filled him, and the feel of Grace's elegant hand in his shot a jolt of electricity sparking up his arm. His visceral response to Grace wasn't for public consumption or hell, even private enjoyment, so he threw on his easy smile. No need for the camera team to highlight his reaction.

During his years in the public eye, he'd honed his laid-back persona because at a young age he'd learned not to allow people to read his true emotions. That skill had helped him survive his childhood with a cheating prick of a dad. And usually, he was chill unless someone was dishonest with him or if he was competing.

In competition mode, his killer instincts rose to the surface. Like today.

A loud whistle filled the air and Betsy spoke. "Great job today. You've got tomorrow off to do whatever you want. We'll have the Jeeps accessible for you if you want to explore the island but there's plenty to see and do on foot. Use the next thirty-six hours to refresh yourselves for the partner competition."

"Will we find out who are partners are tonight?" Melissa asked.

Betsy shook her head. "You'll find out on the morning of Round Two. Don't worry, you will all end up with the partners best suited for the next section of the contest."

"Or the one that makes the best ratings. With my luck, they'll stick me with my ex." Isabella frowned.

Grace turned to her, a crease between her eyebrows. "Your ex?"

Isabella flipped her ponytail over one shoulder. "You don't know?"

"Not all of us watch The Bachelorette," Joey said.

"I knew you'd been a couple before but not the details. Tell us before we head back," Grace said, her voice gentle.

Isabella glanced over at the other team, then lowered her voice. "Well, you people must live under a rock or something. Anyway, I was on Isaac's season of The Bachelor, and he didn't choose me. I ended up coming in third and it was a nightmare. So, I was chosen to be the next Bachelorette and by that time, of course, he and the bimbo he picked had broken up. Sounding familiar yet?"

Toby wasn't alone in shaking his head.

She wrinkled her nose before continuing. "Anyway, the show surprised me on week four by bringing him in to see me. He groveled and apologized and made a huge case for giving him another chance. Like an idiot, I bought it. So, I ended up picking him at the end, we got engaged, and then one month later he informs me he's still in love with the woman he originally chose, and he wanted to try again with her."

"No fucking way. What a dog." Weston glared over at Isaac, who was chatting with Karina.

A hint of sympathy filled Toby. He knew what it felt like to be taken for a ride. Nobody deserved to be treated that way.

Grace rubbed Isabella's shoulder. "And the producers brought you both to compete on this show. Wow, they're diabolical. Did you have any idea?"

Isabella shook her head. "Not a clue. And wouldn't they have fun with making the two of us partners? Makes for great television."

Toby shook his head. "Sorry, Isabella. I don't know if I could have done the show if they'd done something like that to me."

She shrugged. "Well, we're all here for our charities, right? I started mine with my sister to honor our mom who died of a rare type of cancer. So, I can put up with that douche."

Joey patted her on the back, demonstrating he might not be just a brooding drinker. "Sorry again. Okay guys, that was epic. I'm headed back. See you later." He turned on his heel and headed toward the bungalows.

"Me, too. Thanks for listening, I'll see you tonight." Isabella gave a half-wave and she and Weston followed Joey.

Grace met Toby's gaze, her wintry ocean eyes wide. "The plot thickens, right?"

A smile tugged at his lips. "Yeah. Who knows what's going on behind the scenes. Want to walk back?" He could control himself crossing a field with her, right?

She shook her head. "Go ahead. I've got a question for Betsy and then they want to see me in the interview booth."

Disappointment flashed through him but at least she was talking to him again. He shrugged a shoulder. "Sure."

He watched her stride toward the showrunner, unable to resist the temptation of admiring her long muscular legs. Yeah, it was time to be smart and keep his distance. Time to run back to his room and hide from Ms. Grace Steele. Time to get his priorities straight.

CHAPTER 8

*J*nterview Booth: Post-Round One Game Day

"So Grace, congratulations on winning the Highland Games archery and the tug-o-war today. How do you feel?" The monotone voice asked from one of the hidden speakers.

She smiled and responded to the blank wall. "I'm thrilled to have done well in the first round, but I've got to tell you, a spa day would be great right about now."

"Fair point. So tell us how you feel about what happened during the tug-o-war?"

Her belly tightened but she could handle herself in front of a camera. "You mean winning two out of three rounds?"

"No, when Toby asked to switch positions. Earlier in the day, Douglas called you two lovebirds and then you looked upset about the change. Did you two have a spat?"

Every muscle in her body tensed. "You guys are too funny. I just met Toby a few days ago. We're not lovebirds and I wasn't upset about anything except losing the first rope pull. I'm just happy to be here." She smiled wide, but inside she was baring her teeth. Were they frickin' kidding with this?

"Hmmm, we'll take your word for it. Good luck in the next round, Grace."

And the overhead lights came on, signaling the end of another lovely session. Ugh.

~

"OKAY, Toby. Like we said, we knew you'd be the competitor to beat. How does it feel to know you're in the lead after the Highland Games?"

"It feels great, although I'm disappointed I didn't sweep every event." Toby flashed a grin at the blank wall.

"Oh yes, Grace won the archery. But that will keep you on your toes. So why did you make such a big deal about moving away from her during the tug-o-war?"

Toby ground his back molars and shrugged a shoulder. "Hey, part of winning is knowing your weaknesses along with your strengths. I was the weak link in the rear. Weston was better as anchor and I knew if I stayed where I was, I could jeopardize our team's chances." *Though not for the reason you all think.*

"So it wasn't because you two lovebirds weren't getting along?"

Toby's hands curled into fists beneath the table and annoyance flared up his spine. "Like I told you before, Grace and I are just friendly rivals. I'm here to win, nothing more. Anything else?"

"Friendly rivals or lovebirds? I guess we'll all see it unfold. Good luck, Toby."

CHAPTER 9

Grace gazed at the handwritten map one of the producers had given her yesterday evening. The directions to Artemis's Temple seemed straightforward. The goddess had always been her favorite from Greek mythology, especially because of her fierce protection of animals and her skill with a bow and arrow.

No coincidence she'd won the archery competition yesterday––ha ha. She snorted. But seriously, she'd always admired Apollo's twin sister so why wouldn't she take advantage of visiting the ancient temple? It wasn't like she jetted off to the Greek islands on the regular.

The sun peeked out beyond the low mountain ridge, streaking the sky tangerine and lavender and dusky gray. Silky air caressed her skin, and her shoulders softened–– heading out solo was the right move. No cameras here and she'd leave her microphone in the car.

Today's focus was to regroup and mentally prepare herself for the rest of the competition. Not to mention create some space away from Toby. Because it didn't mess with her *at all* that the producers only revealed tomorrow would entail pairs, staggered start times, and up to twelve hours of competition. No clue what would unfold or with whom.

And unless the Universe was messing with her, Toby would *not* be her partner tomorrow.

Yesterday had been...intense. She drummed her fingers on the steering wheel and blew out a frustrated exhale. The day had taken a toll not just on her body but on her mind and heart as well. When Isabella had shared her suspicions the show was throwing her and Isaac together for ratings, it had been a much-needed reminder the show was fake. That she needed to keep her guard up 24/7.

As she'd suspected, Toby's laidback persona had disappeared during the tug-o-war. After they lost the first bout, his first move was to basically throw her under the bus. Like it was all her fault.

How dare he blame her for their loss when he'd been the supposed anchor? Jerk. She hadn't pointed the finger at him. She frowned and gripped the steering wheel tight. Maybe if she hadn't been hyper-aware of the heat of his body mere inches behind her, she could have performed better.

Time to direct her thoughts toward one single purpose: victory. Last night's meditation session had enabled her to wrangle all the external distractions and come back to the reason why she was here. All she needed to do was stick with her practice and avoid Toby. Simple, right?

When she was eight years old, her sitcom mom had taught her to meditate, and she'd been practicing ever since. Back then, meditating helped her learn her lines faster. The child Grace loved the analogy that meditation was learning to "quiet the monkey mind."

She would picture her brain as a windowless room with a troop of wild monkeys in play mode--zooming around, bouncing off the walls, distracting her from finding a sense of calm. Meditation was teaching your personal troop of monkeys that being distracted all the time isn't how you want to experience your life. Easier said than done but a girl could try.

The curved road narrowed to a single lane and an enormous crooked tree appeared at the peak of the hill. The directions indicated to turn left at the landmark, and she swung the wheel sharply. Within seconds, an oasis unfolded before her. Her throat tightened as she scanned the scene, complete with what must be Artemis's Temple, with a stone floor framed by thick columns.

Endless emerald fields of scarlet poppies fluttered in the wind. Low stone walls stretched toward the horizon, dotted with stone columns extending up toward the blue bowl of sky. She'd never witnessed anything so beautiful in her life.

She parked the Jeep in a small clearing. Entranced, she hurried to the temple, a swirl of warm wind lifting her hair off her shoulders. Maybe she'd been drawn here to implore Artemis to bestow some of her grace and courage upon her.

Something about this place had her blood humming through her veins. She returned to the Jeep and grabbed her backpack filled with snacks and water. Plenty of time to hike later, for now, she'd sit and soak it all in. She located a carved stone bench, tucked her legs beneath her, and scanned the view. Just beyond the flower-covered fields, the azure waters of the Ionian shimmered.

If she couldn't reset her mood and access her resilience here, it wasn't happening. She savored the ocean air and the preternatural quiet. Heaven.

And then the sound of wheels crunching on gravel alerted her she was no longer alone. She turned to see Toby cruising in on a mountain bike. Because of course, of all the rivals to invade her solitude, it had to be him. She swallowed a scream because there was no avoiding him now.

He took his time with the kickstand and removed his

helmet, revealing disheveled russet hair that gleamed like fire in the morning light. Since he'd cycled up the hill, his muscles shone with a fine sheen of sweat, emphasizing his lean muscular frame. He lifted one long-fingered hand in a wave and sauntered toward the temple. Her blood heated and not with passion.

"Did the producers have you follow me up here?" What was the deal with this guy being everywhere? Especially after how he'd acted yesterday.

He shook his head and approached. "Of course I didn't follow you up here. Someone mentioned this spot last night at dinner. I didn't know you'd be here. I was actually taking some alone time."

She pointed at her chest. "Well, I got here first and I'm taking some solo time. So hop back on your bike and pedal somewhere else." Yes, she was acting more like a nine-year-old than a twenty-nine-year-old but enough was enough.

Toby sighed and scrubbed his hands through his already messy hair. "Grace."

She narrowed her eyes. "Toby."

He dropped down beside her. "Look, let's clear the air. I think you misunderstood why I wanted to switch up the line yesterday."

She huffed out a breath. "Oh really? I misunderstood? Because it seemed crystal clear you were blaming me for being the weak link during the tug-o-war."

He shook his head. "That's not it. I——"

"Come on Toby. It was obvious. I know I'm not a professional athlete like you but there were five of us and you called me out in front of the cameras. Look, it hurt my feelings, okay?" She struggled to slow down her breathing because her pulse was hammering in her throat.

"It was a simple strategy to rearrange our team. We won,

right? You're taking this too personally." His gaze dropped to his knees, so close to her own.

"Of course I wanted to win--this competition is personal for all of us, right? So please, can you allow me to enjoy the temple by myself for a few hours? I need some space. And you still haven't apologized."

He turned to her, a flicker of regret shadowing his green eyes. "Grace, I'm sorry."

"You sound sincere, but it doesn't explain why you singled me out. What's the real story?" And why did it hurt?

He squeezed his eyes closed for a moment and blew out a noisy exhale. "Fine, you want to know why I needed you to move? Because I couldn't concentrate with you so close to me, okay?"

Her throat tightened. "What do you mean?"

"What do you think I mean? I think you're fucking gorgeous and all I wanted to do was drop that rope and get my hands all over you. If I hadn't gotten away from you, we would have lost. Okay?" He rose and stalked away from her.

Heat rose in her cheeks, and she couldn't help but check out the way his shorts hugged his narrow hips and perfect butt. "So you're saying you wanted me to move because you were turned on?"

He kept his gaze on the horizon and spoke over his shoulder. "It's pretty obvious I'm attracted to you. But I'm not going to mess up either of our chances of winning and that's where things were headed if I'd stayed in the line behind you."

"Oh." She blew out a breath. So the sparks dancing between them weren't just her imagination.

"Yeah, oh." He pivoted back toward her and flashed his crooked grin. "Forgive me?"

Her heart took a rolling tumble in her chest. The guy was

way too appealing, despite being an admitted flirt and charmer.

Hooking up with him, although tempting, was too much of a distraction. She couldn't think clearly around him. And she'd learned her lesson about what a bad idea it was to trust and get close to people in show business. Once burned and all that.

She'd play it cool. She stood and walked over to him. "You're forgiven but don't pull that kind of thing on me again, okay?"

He held out one strong hand. "Let's shake on it. But when the show is finished and we're back in California, can I take you to dinner?"

Her breath caught in her throat, but she extended her hand and placed it in his. Rough calluses teased her skin and a quick flare of heat rushed through her. What would those strong hands feel like skimming along her skin?

"Maybe. Why don't we talk about it after I win? My victory might change your mind." She flashed her own self-satisfied grin--she could handle one charming player.

His pupils flared, leaving only a halo of green. With a quick tug, he pulled her into the circle of his powerful arms, his tempting lips inches from her own. She sucked in a sharp inhale.

"Can I kiss you?" His voice was raspy, sexier than hell.

Her arms wound around his neck of their own volition, caught in the snare of his gaze. If he didn't kiss her right this second, she'd tug his head down because Toby McAvoy was impossible to resist. "Please."

He wrapped her ponytail in one fist, held her in place, and captured her mouth. Passion flared between them, and a moan escaped her. She slid her hands into his wavy hair, tugging him closer. His other hand slid down to her butt and yanked her against him, leaving no doubt he was as turned on as she was. Tongues tangled and stroked, and heat curled down her spine. He nipped her lower lip, then soothed it with his tongue before diving deep again. A moan escaped her.

Ohmygod, Toby "Fox" McAvoy was the best kisser she'd ever met. The sparks from the past few days detonated and she melted against his lean, hard body. She couldn't get enough of his delicious cinnamon taste and the scent of soap and clean sweat on his skin.

He lifted his head and dropped his forehead against hers, his breath coming in harsh pants, matching the wild thrumming of her heart.

He exhaled an unsteady breath and stepped back with a wicked grin. "If you'll kiss me like that again, maybe which one of us wins won't matter."

She pressed her fingers against her lips, swollen and tender from the firm pressure of his mouth. Yeah, she didn't have a quick comeback. Nor a quick recovery. Not after that earth-shattering kiss. Holy crap was she in trouble.

"But I know you want some alone time and I think it's smarter for both of us if I find another spot. I'll see you back at the estate. Think about dinner." With a wink, he turned and sauntered back to his bike.

She backed up a few steps, her knees buckled, and she dropped onto the stone seat. The only way she'd survive and win this competition was to keep her distance from Toby. This time for real. Because now that she'd had a sweet, delicious taste of him?

Next time she might be the one who pounced, and she didn't think she'd be able to stop with just a kiss. And if he was playing up the attraction as part of his game strategy?

She was in more trouble than she'd realized.

CHAPTER 10

ension was tangible in the air--Toby wasn't the only one battling nerves. It wasn't like the anxiety he'd feel before a big snowboarding competition or anything. But between the mind-blowing kiss yesterday and the resulting two cold showers, two unsatisfying bouts with his hand, topped off by a sleepless night, his gut was churning.

And that didn't even factor in what fresh hell would be in store for them today in the partner competition.

Once again, he had maneuvered his position as far away from Grace as possible. But of course her shiny ponytail and white tank top were visible out of the corner of his eye. The woman made him forget why he was even doing this show. Avoidance was best. He could deal with the tightening in his chest every time he was close to her later. Like on the flight home after he'd won.

Frances stepped onto the dais sporting a classic Greek toga. Playing it up for the cameras capturing the scene from every angle of the courtyard. She was going to give one of them one million dollars so as far as he was concerned, she could wear whatever the hell she wanted.

"Good morning, warriors! Today, you and a partner will be navigating my twenty-acre hedge labyrinth, which was modeled after the 'Labyrinth of Love.' It was one of the most famous ones built at Villa Pisani in Italy outside of Verona. Napoleon bought it for his adoptive son the Viceroy of Italy. Unlike the classical labyrinth, which is a unicursal walking path with one route to the center, this one has multicursal paths with branching patterns that require decisions.

"You and your partner will enter the maze at staggered times and have up to twelve hours to cross the finish line. The winning team will be the one who reaches the tower building in the center and exits the labyrinth in the shortest time frame."

Everyone began shouting at once and Frances held up a hand. "Hold on, let me finish. Your headlamp will have a camera, cameras are strategically placed throughout the hedges, and drones will also be capturing footage. There are three small stone structures and the large tower in the center. Each one is equipped with water and bathroom facilities."

"When do we start?" Grace called from the other side of the group.

He glanced over at her, and her beauty struck him in the solar plexus. Unlike the furrowed brows and frowns on the other competitors' faces, Grace merely smiled up at their host. The woman sure could keep her emotions close to the vest, which was to her advantage in the contest.

After yesterday's kiss, he wasn't sure how he felt about her poker face personally. Sure, she seemed genuine, but she had been a famous actor and wasn't acting a big game of pretend? And he had a history of being attracted to women who weren't honest. How could he trust whether Grace's reactions to him were real or for the camera? Even though yesterday's encounter hadn't been caught on camera. He hoped.

Betsy laughed. "Great attitude, Grace. Get ready for the most unique experience of your life, everyone."

The showrunner handed Frances an enormous cream-colored envelope with one of those old-fashioned wax seals. Frances carefully opened it and slid out a square card with gold gilt edges.

Toby ran his tongue around his teeth. Oh shit, he had a feeling…he looked at Grace and her hands were clasped, her full lips pressed into a tight line. Was she anxious, too?

"Very well. Here are the teams and start times. Team #1 is Toby and Grace. Team #2 is Weston and Karina. Team #3 is Clay and Joey. Team #4 is Melissa and Kimmelle. And Team #5 is Isabella and Isaac, who will be the last team to enter the labyrinth. You have thirty minutes to report to the Jeeps, which will transport you out to the labyrinth where provisions await. Got it?"

For a moment, a hush hung thick in the balmy island air.

"May I speak to you for a minute privately before we do anything else?" Isaac's usually smooth baritone was high-pitched and strained.

"Me, too. I thought we'd be paired up boy/girl. There's gotta be a mistake," Clay grumbled.

Frances's eyes narrowed a fraction, and she held up a hand, in a now familiar gesture. "Isaac, if your question pertains to your partner, the answer is no. If you are having some type of personal emergency that requires medical or psychiatric care, then the answer is yes. I'm sorry you made assumptions based on gender, Clayton, but there are valid reasons for each pairing."

An uncomfortable silence filled the courtyard.

Toby made sure his expression remained smooth--no chance he could ask for another partner. Although inside, he was freaking out. How the hell could he handle twelve hours in a giant fucking shrubbery with Grace and stay focused on the prize? Shit, shit, and double shit.

Had the producers noticed their chemistry? They had certainly paired them up every opportunity they had--the Jeep, dinner, the tug-o-war, and now the partner competition. Maybe there had been hidden cameras at the temple yesterday revealing his and Grace's kiss? And he'd do well not to forget that although this competition might be for a good cause, at the end of the day, the producers wanted dramatic storylines and high ratings. Period.

"Good luck and I'll look forward to following your progress and congratulating the winning team this evening. Remember that while being an excellent competitor is important to really make a difference in the world--as all of you are with your respective charities--teamwork is imperative.

"Regardless of your personal feelings toward a partner or co-worker, learning to play well with others is a key component in success." Frances smiled and exited the dais.

He snorted and rolled his eyes. Yeah, because playing with Grace was the problem.

CHAPTER 11

"How far away is this labyrinth?" Grace asked Sara, the story producer transporting her and Toby to the site.

"It's about another twenty minutes and you aren't mic'd until we arrive. Just enjoy the scenery."

They were cruising in the same direction she'd driven to see the Temple of Artemis. In the backseat, she could appreciate the hairpin turns and breathtaking sea views as they traversed up the steep hilly roads. The sun shone, the breeze whistled, and the island felt like some type of Utopia.

Well, except for sitting next to Toby and being dropped into some crazy hedge and having to escape. Despite meditating during their thirty minute reprieve, her heart galloped against her ribcage and her body pounded with adrenaline. Yeah, full fight-or-flight mode.

This show was becoming one big exercise in revealing how little self-control she had. After yesterday, they needed to figure out how to work together today without letting the pesky panties-on-fire chemistry between them derail their desires.

She peeked at Toby, but he was staring out at the passing landscape. Twenty minutes without cameras was an opportunity they couldn't blow, especially since they were heading into the maze first.

She reached for his sinewy forearm, and he jumped. His skin was warm, and the sprinkling of hair was crisp beneath her fingers.

She snatched her hand back and clasped hers together in her lap. "Sorry, I didn't mean to startle you."

A smile tugged at his chiseled mouth. "Just trying to wrap my head around this labyrinth. Any ideas?"

She wrinkled her nose. "Same. Okay, who knew this information would come in handy one day, but I just so happen to know that labyrinths are often associated with spiritual journeys. Cathedrals, like Chartres in France, have a labyrinth inlaid into the floor. Books and movies tend to portray labyrinths as journeys of self-reflection and growth. A labyrinth has no dead ends, just choices of pathways and results of those decisions…"

He nodded. "Look at you, the labyrinth scholar. It makes sense, though––Frances wants us to learn something about ourselves. But I can't figure out why they keep pairing us up. I mean, some pairs are obvious like, maybe Clay and Joey will brawl or something which would be good for ratings? But why us?"

She inhaled a steadying breath. "Us? Well, it feels like they are angling for some kind of showmance. Do you think there were hidden cameras at the temple yesterday?"

"Shit, you're probably right. And the Highland Games guy made a point to call us lovebirds." He rubbed a hand along the scruff on his chiseled jaw.

"Well, we can't control how they edit us. All we can do is focus on winning this challenge. I promise I'll give 100% and will have your back. Deal?"

He flashed a grin and extended a hand. "I'm in. Shake on it?"

"Just the shake, though." She slid her hand into his square-palmed one and tingles danced up her arm.

Yeah, the flashback to him taking charge and holding her head in place when he kissed her was visceral. With control, she released his hand. No more touching or she was in trouble. His kissing skills were romance-novel hero worthy.

He looked down, massaged the back of his neck, then gazed up at her. "So, are we cool?"

Cool was a complete 180 from what they were but she could handle it. She ran her tongue around her teeth. "Fine. We're fine."

"Since we're in the Jeep for a little longer, can I ask why you left Hollywood?"

"So you don't remember hearing all the stories?"

He shook his head. "I don't but I wasn't allowed to watch much TV and spent most of my time on the slopes. I'd heard of your show, *Molly's World*, right? Fill me in."

Why not? "Okay, I played Molly, the lead from *Molly's World*, from the time I was seven until I was thirteen. Umm… let's just say things basically ended when I hit puberty."

"What changed?" His tone gentled, as if he could read between the lines of what she wasn't saying.

She sighed. "Me. I changed. I played a ballerina and when I turned thirteen, suddenly I wasn't this petite little girl. They said I looked too mature for the part. My mom, who was my manager, was the first one to criticize me when I got boobs––like I could control my body. She made me bind them so the producers wouldn't notice.

"My supposed best friend Brittany, who was also on the show, told them. They wrote me out and gave her the lead. They even changed the name to *Carrie's World*, because that was her character's name."

"Doesn't sound like much of a best friend. And you didn't want to do more TV or movies?"

She shrugged. "After my mother and Brittany basically stole the lead from me, I didn't want to be in that world anymore. And the audience saw me as Molly. So many child actors can't escape that first role. Not all of us are Miley Cyrus leaving Hannah Montana."

His brows drew together. "Wait, what? Your mother?"

"Yeah, she managed my career and Brittany's. And she backed Brittany instead of me..." She exhaled a steadying breath--sometimes the betrayal still hurt.

He whistled through his teeth. "Grace, that sucks. It sounds toxic. So you haven't acted since then?"

"Nope, I swore I'd never be on television again, but my sanctuary needs a big infusion of cash fast, so I took a gamble."

"Not to be rude but I thought sitcoms paid a lot. Can you use any of that money?"

She snorted. "They do and I had a great nest egg, but my mother controlled it until I turned eighteen. And in the process, she spent most of it. After college and starting Golden Years Pet Sanctuary, there wasn't much left."

"Grace, I'm so sorry. I think what you're doing is amazing." He massaged her shoulder, and it was her turn to jump because his touch sent an immediate flush of heat through her.

She forced her voice to remain even despite the way her pulse kicked up. "Everyone has a story, right? We've all been through something that made us into who we are today, for better or for worse."

"That's true. But before I forget, tell me where I can watch *Molly's World*. I need to see if you learned that pirouette when you were a kid, you know the one you used with the hammer throw."

She rolled her eyes and laughed. "Ha ha. No way. If you don't know, I'm not telling you."

"I have my ways." He rubbed his hands together like an old-time movie villain.

Toby's humor had a way of lightening her mood and didn't that make him even more appealing? The Jeep slowed and Grace looked up. Sara pulled into a narrow gravel road, framed by towering Cypress trees.

"Well, you're sharing something about your past with me once we're in the labyrinth. Only fair. And it looks like it's almost showtime." She swallowed the nerves fluttering up her throat.

"Yeah, and we'll have everyone chasing us down––no pressure." Toby rolled his shoulders.

The Jeep bumped and rocked along the increasingly rutted road. Like Frances's estate, the lane opened to a large clearing. The vast area resembled much of the island with its low stone walls, clumps of trees, and fields of poppies spread out to the horizon.

The property was bustling with activity. Several crew members were unloading equipment from two shiny white trucks. Grace shaded her eyes from the metallic glare of the camera operators filming their arrival and surveyed the scene.

Several drones squatted on a drop-cloth apparently awaiting activation. A twinge of familiarity shot through her––she'd spent her entire childhood on television sets and sometimes she missed the excitement and commotion. Regretted the way it had ended.

No time for regrets now. Time to focus on the labyrinth challenge.

Toby whistled and pointed a finger in the opposite direction. "Check that out. Those look like the movie version of

Heaven's Gate or something. And that's Frances wearing a toga again."

She turned and laughed at the ornate golden gates. "Right? Those are like thirty feet high. Maybe an angel's going to float down to greet us or something. And I guess Frances is opening the gates for us."

"Yep. And they're probably real gold. I guess we should be glad they aren't spiked black iron and look like the entrance to Hell."

They both stared at the closed entrance, which was framed by high emerald green hedges that spanned out in each direction. Tops of what appeared to be stone towers or buildings were visible beyond the greenery, but the gates were so thick that no path was detectable. At least from the parking lot view anyway.

A chill shot down her spine and goosebumps rose on her skin. Weird--it was sunny and 70 degrees. This was *not* a Stephen King novel and Jack Nicholson was not in that maze. Her imagination wasn't doing her any favors today. She rubbed her bare arms and redirected her attention back to Toby.

Together, they crossed the gravel lot to where Betsy was waving her arms at them. "Team #1, come on down and get your provisions. You're up."

Toby caught her hand and together they sauntered to the supply table as if they didn't have a care in the world. The cameras were rolling, and they would present a united front. After she'd shared the details of her past with him, he'd been sweet and supportive. She hadn't told many people about her mother's betrayal, but somehow she'd felt comfortable enough to share with Toby.

One of the producers helped them put on their medium-sized backpacks, complete with a small bedroll. Yeah, because they'd have plenty of time to take a nap.

"Okay you two, follow me over to the entrance. Double-check your mics, please." Betsy marched toward the golden gates, and they trailed behind her.

Grace's pulse thundered in her temples, and she slowed down her breathing, forcing herself to extend her exhales and regulate her racing heart. Time to be strong and steady and a good partner for Toby.

One of the videographers followed their progress. They reached the imposing wrought iron barrier and Frances whipped out a giant golden key. She slid it into the keyhole and turned. The gates glided silently open and a wide corridor, lined with greenery, appeared. Dappled sunlight bounced off the smooth stone footpath and the reflection of a camera high in the dense foliage reminded her they would be filmed the entire time. Toby nudged her and Grace turned to him, meeting his wide eyes with her own stunned expression.

"Incredible, right? The initial portion, which you can see now, is a straight shot and then the paths begin branching off. This is the only entrance and the only exit. You two ready?" Frances scanned both their faces and they nodded.

"Excellent, now please set the watches we gave you. The timers are set at twelve hours, and they are programmed to count down, so you'll know how much time you have at any given moment."

Grace and Toby both tapped their large diver-style watches. The screen illuminated with the neon-orange digital timer. Although Toby's expression appeared calm, the set of his shoulders revealed she wasn't the only anxious one. With the camera guy capturing everything close-up, she retreated behind her poker face.

Frances snagged each of their hands and lifted their arms high––yeah, not over the top at all––and bellowed, "Team #1, go."

Their host stepped back, and she and Toby entered the labyrinth. The gate slammed shut behind them, the click of the key turning in the lock a dramatic footnote.

No turning back now.

CHAPTER 12

Toby matched his pace to Grace's long-legged stride. With each step deeper into the labyrinth, external sounds dropped away, and silence settled around them. The hedge walls towered on each side until the lane ended in a three-way split.

She stopped and placed her hands on her hips. "So, every one of these paths look identical. It's possible all of them are correct or two could be dead ends, I don't know."

He rubbed his jaw and contemplated their choices. "Okay labyrinth expert, any ideas?"

She frowned and stared up at the sky. "Well, we need to make it to the center tower. We can track our progress with the sun and right now it's up in the east. I say we go west. I mean, ancient civilizations used the sun and planets for everything, right?" She pointed to the one branching off to the left.

He huffed out a breath. This challenge was ridiculous. Hell, Daedalus couldn't get out of the maze he'd created for the Minotaur in Crete. So how were they supposed to figure it out?

"I don't know about going west but it's as good an idea as any." Not like he had anything better.

After about ten minutes, the path narrowed, and the light faded. The top branches now formed a canopy, shrouding the path in shadow. So much for following the sun.

He stopped and blew out a breath. "Hold on. This feels wrong. I know we're supposed to find the center, but I can't see a damn thing. We need to figure out how far down each path we'll go before turning around. Otherwise, we'll never get out of here, much less win."

She poked a finger against his chest. "Well, any brilliant ideas? Do we keep going in this direction or do we go back?"

He gritted his teeth and tried to ignore how even the touch of one of Grace's elegant fingertips caused every muscle in his body to tighten. Damn it, even an innocent touch drove him wild, which the cameras interspersed through the maze probably caught clearly.

He stepped back, putting some space between them. A safety net.

He forced a relaxed grin. "How about we pick a time frame, like fifteen minutes, and we'll check in if the path feels off, like this one."

She waved a hand. "Okay. We do have headlamps if it stays dark, but I don't have a good feeling about this path. Maybe it's all a giant mind-game. Like, they want us to give up and turn back and want to see if we persevere."

He retreated a step so he could use his brain without it being clouded by the sweet scent of her long hair. "That's the thing. Are we overthinking it and this is just a dead end, and they want us to waste time or is it something more?"

She gave a quick nod. "Exactly. If we keep with the idea that labyrinths are spiritual journeys, no way would Frances make it an easy straightforward path without twists and turns. So do we turn around or keep going?"

"I like the way you think. Five more minutes and we turn back. Deal?" Grace was insightful and that intrigued him.

As suspected, the path was a dead end with a camera lens sticking out of the top of the hedge. Probably to catch their disappointed expressions. They turned around and headed back.

"Okay, confession time. I get a little claustrophobic in enclosed spaces like this. I need a distraction from these creepy thick branches. It's your turn to share something real. Why did you quit competing? Did you age out or something?" Grace asked.

"Age out? No, but my good friend was badly injured when we were off riding some back trails and after that, I just couldn't keep my mind in the game." Couldn't shake the guilt that Josh was paralyzed, and he'd walked away without a bruise or scrape.

She stopped and turned, and he bumped into her again. "Oh my god, Toby, that's awful. Is your friend okay?"

He sucked in a sharp inhale. "No, Josh is a paraplegic now and he's the reason I started the Alpine Adaptive Athlete Foundation."

"I'm so sorry. I think it's amazing you've helped your friend and so many other people. Do you still snowboard?" She placed one cool hand on his shoulder.

He stiffened and retreated a step. A small crease formed between her brows and her hand dropped by her side. "Yeah, I love the mountains, so I just go for fun. Probably why I've lost my competitive edge."

"Oh please. You're hands down the top contestant here. And I'm glad the experience didn't completely ruin your passion." She bit her lip.

Her plump pink lower lip that he'd sunk his teeth into yesterday. Yeah, his passion for her wasn't diminishing. *Act cool.*

He shrugged and tapped his watch. "We better keep going. Let's try one of the other paths, pronto." Needed to stop revisiting the past and focus on not pouncing on Grace.

"Right, let's go." She turned and took off at a trot.

When they reached the intersection, they contemplated the two remaining paths. Once again, Toby had no clue which one to choose--this maze was legit.

Light bounced off yet another camera positioned above them, high up in the hedge. Frances hadn't exaggerated when she said they were everywhere. But he'd take it over a cameraperson following them.

Grace spun in a circle. "I know which way I think we should go but what do you think? And should we use the string they gave us to mark our path? In case we get turned around?"

"Let's go that way." He pointed to the path closest to Grace. "Zero clue if it was right or wrong. And no to the string because what if one of the other teams sees it and takes it or uses it as a shortcut?"

She beamed at him. "That's the one I wanted so it's got to be right if we both chose it. Why don't you lead this time and I'll set the timer on my watch.

Perfect. Now he could focus on the trail and not watch the sway of Grace's hips. "Done. If either of us are going to win this competition, we need to find the center of the labyrinth."

A thrashing sound came from behind them. "Oh shit, do you think that's one of the other teams? I don't want anyone to get ahead of us. You up for a little jog?"

"Absolutely. Let's go." She gave a thumbs up and they took off running.

The corridor grew curvier with short separate hedges popping up left and right. But the path remained wide, and when they rounded a sharp corner, they came upon a small stone tower, complete with a bubbling fountain, and flowering vines stretching up to the top.

He leaned forward, placing his hands on his thighs. "Okay, I think we lost them, and this is incredible. It must mean we're on the right track, right?"

Grace tilted her head as she approached the stairs leading up to an arched doorway. "Well, there's a bathroom in there so I'll consider it a win either way. But, yes, this is beautiful."

Just like you. "Bathroom is good. Meet me at the top of the tower, we'll be able to see the one in the center and figure out our next move."

"I'll meet you up there. I mean, since there are four separate paths, anything could give us an advantage." She hurried through the doorway.

He ascended a curving staircase on the far side of the structure. Thank god they wouldn't have to try to scale the vines or anything like that. Time for some water and a snack. He climbed to the top and took off his backpack and his mic--the producers didn't need to listen to him eating.

And damn if his guard hadn't relaxed around Grace. Especially after her opening up on the ride over about her childhood and how her mom had screwed her over? Trusting people didn't come easy for him but something about her told him she was genuine. Her story had touched his heart and damn if she didn't deserve a break.

It sounded like her animal rescue was her whole life and after what she'd been through? His earlier doubts about her honesty had evaporated with each turn through the maze. So what happened after they won the labyrinth together? Only one of them could win the prize money if they were the last two standing.

And he owed it to his athletes to win this competition.

CHAPTER 13

Grace smoothed her hair back from her face and scaled the winding steps to meet Toby. She hadn't shared the story of how Brittany and her mom had betrayed her in a long time. Sharing it with Toby had been surprisingly easy and hadn't evoked the embarrassment the memories usually triggered.

How refreshing to be real with him. Instead of him looking at her with pity, he'd acted impressed with her strength. And his sweet attempts to get her to laugh had warmed her heart. Why, why, why was the universe so perverse to put Toby in her orbit now?

Dating in L.A. was a shit show, especially for an introverted former actress. Running a rescue was emotionally all-consuming. At the end of the day, she usually couldn't muster the energy to socialize with her friends, much less a significant other. Toby was the first guy she could be herself with in what felt like eons.

And he'd revealed his compassionate heart. His foundation was changing lives and had such a personal basis.

Distress had colored his tone when he discussed his friend's accident. Talk about a lot to shoulder.

She rounded the corner and there he was, leaning against the turret wall surveying his domain, looking all sexy and brooding.

"Figured it out yet? I can't see any other towers, so that's out the window."

His solemn expression morphed into what she was beginning to recognize as his signature happy-go-lucky grin. His lean face grew more handsome each moment she spent with him. And the mouth on him was simply dangerous.

"Let's take five. I took off my mic—-no need for them to hear us chewing." He handed her a protein bar. "We've got to keep our energy up. And we've had luck taking the paths to the left so why don't we keep doing that?"

She removed her mic and peeled open the wrapper. "Sounds good. And maybe you'll tell me about your tattoos?" She'd been intrigued by his full sleeve from the moment she noticed it on the plane.

He shrugged. "Sure. The first one is for the Three Muske-teers, my two best friends and I got it back when we were teenagers. The fleur-de-lis, the sword, and the diamond symbolize we were inseparable."

"I love it. And are you guys still inseparable?" The meaning behind the ink was as beautiful as the artwork. And it only served to highlight his muscular forearms.

He nodded. "Yeah, but now Olivia and Grant are getting married. Things changed about a year ago, but we're still all best friends, even though sometimes I feel like a third wheel."

"I bet but I'm sure they don't feel that way. And the Olympic rings are self-explanatory and the fox, since you shared that nickname. But what's the hawk for?"

His nostrils flared. "That's for Josh. It was his nickname when he competed because his focus was so powerful. And the cliff and waves represent the California coast and remind me how the sea helps me chill out."

Unable to help herself, she stroked one hand along his firm, defined arm. "I love that they all have so much significance for you. They're amazing." *You're amazing.*

He hissed and stepped away from her. "Grace."

"Sorry." She yanked her hand back like she'd been burned. Heat flooded her cheeks. Damn it, why couldn't she keep her hands off him?

In the tight corridors of the maze, his proximity amplified her attraction and the more he shared about himself, the more her initial chemical reaction grew. It was more than physical now.

He grabbed his mic and backpack and turned. "I'm going to hit the bathroom and we should get going. Meet me downstairs in two." With that, he disappeared down the stairs.

Great. Now she'd chased him off. Be professional, Grace. Remember what's at stake.

If she didn't win, her life as she knew it would be dramatically transformed. And she couldn't even imagine what she'd do about the animals she'd already committed to finding homes. After the competition, if Toby had been serious about going to dinner in California, she could explore their attraction then.

Not now. How tough could it be to resist him?

Over the next six and a half hours, it proved exceptionally frickin' difficult. But they managed to navigate the twists and turns in mostly companionable silence. They worked great together as a team and agreed to every new choice together.

She trusted his judgment and he had a contagious air of confidence about him. Toby McAvoy was the whole package. Maybe something real besides the prize money could come out of this reality show?

They reached another intersection and paused to assess their next move. Her pulse kicked up--her intuition was screaming that they were close. "I think it's to the right. I think we're here."

"Yeah, I feel it, too. And you're right, look where the sun is now that it's afternoon. We are west."

Anticipation fueled their steps and once again, they were bounding down the path together. When they rounded the corner, there it was: the big beautiful central tower--the symbol they'd arrived.

Toby pumped his arms in the air. "Yes, we did it. And in less than eight hours."

A joyous laugh escaped her. "Because we are #1. No way will anybody else be able to match our pace. Woohoo! Let's go get that letter."

"We are #1. You're #1. We did it." He caught her hand and sparks danced along her skin. They sprinted up the stone steps to the entrance.

They entered the wide doorway into a white marble vestibule. Gorgeous statues of goddesses dominated the corners and magnificent murals of pristine blue sky and white-capped waves adorned the walls. In the center of the space, a stack of large cream-colored envelopes sat on a pedestal.

She gasped and pressed one hand to her pounding heart. "Wow, it's like we've stepped into a museum. This is incredible."

Toby crossed to the dais, grabbed the envelope bearing their names, and tore it open. He scanned the document and roared with laughter.

She crossed the mosaic-tiled floor to his side. "It's funny?"

"Read it." He thrust the paper at her. It was a map of the labyrinth with a few words along the top for them.

"*Congratulations Grace and Toby. If you're reading this, you made it to the center in the allotted time. As a reward, this map will show a direct route to the exit. A car will be awaiting you and will transport you back to the estate. The winning team will be announced tomorrow. Good job, Frances Ellis."*

"I'd say it's hilarious we spent almost eight hours getting here and this path out looks like it's a straight shot that will take an hour or so." Toby chuckled again.

Her lips twitched. "Right? I'll take it. I'm ready, let's go."

They hurried outside and her joy couldn't be repressed. "We did it."

She tossed her backpack before executing a few perfect pirouettes down the stairs. Yeah, she still had moves.

"There's my ballerina." Toby dropped his pack, picked her up by her waist, and swung her in a circle.

The moment his strong hands spanned her waist and pulled her closer, their jubilance transformed. Excitement tingled along her skin and heat bloomed low in her belly. She wrapped her legs around his narrow hips, clasped his face in her hands, and planted a kiss on his lips.

He groaned and slid his hands down to her butt, tugging her closer against the steel ridge of his erection. She rocked against him, savoring the solid feel of his hot hard body.

"Grace," he rasped against her lips before diving in, his tongue swirling and stroking against hers.

Somehow his breath still had a faint hint of cinnamon mingled with a taste that was uniquely his--a little tart, a little spicy. She dug her fingers into his thick hair and strained closer. Her nipples pebbled, and her skin tingled.

He broke the kiss and gazed up at her. "You are the most beautiful woman I've ever seen." He trailed his fingers down her shoulder and goosebumps rose along her skin.

"You're not so bad yourself."

He tugged her hair from its ponytail, and it fell in a curtain around them. Their bodies fit together like two puzzle pieces, lining up like they were made for each other. Time fell away and only sensation remained. The warmth from the sun on her skin, the feel of his lips against hers.

A buzzing sound filtered into her awareness. She lifted her head and glanced around.

Toby cursed and released her. "Fuck, there's a drone right above us."

Her legs trembled and her cheeks burned. "I can't believe we forgot about all the cameras."

She gathered her hair back into a messy ponytail and scanned the area. Of course there had to be several cameras positioned around the labyrinth's center. They'd allowed their excitement to blur their judgment.

And now the producers had gotten their showmance on film. She could potentially be a celebrity joke, like she'd been as a kid. Damn it.

Toby picked up their backpacks. "We should head to the car. Are you okay?"

"Depending on how much they caught on film, it's kind of my worst nightmare but it's not your fault. I kissed you. When they have us in the interview rooms later, we can just say we got caught up in the moment, right? Maybe it was only the drone and that was overhead. Maybe there weren't any close-ups."

He caught her hands in his. He dropped his forehead against hers and she inhaled a steadying breath. This guy with his tender gestures and hot moves tugged at her heart.

"Maybe we'll get lucky." He lifted his head, placed his hand over his mic, and gazed deep into her eyes. "Cover your mic for a second, I need to ask you something. Can I come to your room tonight? I don't want to wait until we get back to California to be with you."

Her throat tightened and despite the drone ice bucket,

her heart kicked against her ribs. "Yes, absolutely yes. No cameras there, right?"

His green eyes gleamed. "No cameras. Just you and me."

"What are we waiting for? Let's go."

They sprinted away from the tower.

CHAPTER 14

fter dinner, they half-jogged down the estate's pathway, careful to maintain arm's distance but the heat sparking between them probably blazed like a beacon. Grace didn't care. When they reached their bungalows, Toby glanced around and nodded. With a giggle, she veered toward him and together they tumbled into his suite.

He slammed the door and backed her against it. He slid his hands into her hair, holding her in place, then swooped in and claimed her mouth. His tongue stroked and tangled with hers, his breath warm and delicious. She wound her arms around his neck and melted against his carved from marble body. When his impressive erection lined up with her center, her legs went weak. Without the wooden door behind her, she'd collapse.

His hands roamed down her sides, sparking heat along her skin, and she pressed closer. Wanting more. A sigh escaped her when he caught her breast, brushing his thumb across her taut nipple.

He broke the kiss and trailed his lips down her neck, then his mouth closed over the sensitive peak through the thin material of her top. When he used his teeth, sparks jolted straight to her center. Her head lolled back against the door, and she rocked her hips against his hard length, savoring the friction.

Closer, she needed to get closer.

She grabbed his shirt and yanked, desperate to feel his bare skin. He shifted back and tugged off the t-shirt, tossing it aside. She stroked both hands along his defined pecs, his carved from marble eight-pack, and those sharp V's disappearing into his shorts.

His skin was impossibly soft over the rigid lines of his lean muscles. His body was gorgeous and athletic. She traced one finger along the light trail of hair leading to the waistband of his shorts, and he sucked in a harsh breath.

Their eyes locked, his moss green eyes hooded, the pupils flared. "You are the sexiest woman I've ever met."

"Kiss me." More, all she could think of was *more*.

With a growl, he slanted his mouth against hers, and she sank into the sensation of his tongue swirling and stroking with hers. Yeah, he tasted even better than he looked.

"Hold onto my shoulders," he rasped against her mouth.

She shifted her arms around his neck again and sank against the door.

"I've got you." He dropped to his knees and pulled off her yoga capris and thong and pitched them aside. He slid his calloused palms up from her knees, spreading her apart, so she was open to his gaze.

Her breath caught in her throat, but she couldn't look away. "Toby, please."

He stroked one long finger against her and groaned. "You're soaked. Is this all for me?"

Oh my god, he was a talker. "Yes," she managed.

"So fucking beautiful. Spread wider for me." He nudged her legs further apart, without lifting his head.

"Please." If he didn't touch her or kiss her now, she was going to lose it.

"Look at me." His voice was a husky growl.

She gazed down and he was looking up at her, his eyes hooded, his chiseled mouth parted. Her breath caught and a shiver shot down her spine.

"I want you to watch me while I kiss you and lick you until you come apart on my tongue." He leaned in and licked her in one long stroke, and her legs trembled but he held her thighs apart, pinning her to the door.

She dropped her hands to his head and dug her fingers into his thick wavy hair.

He licked and kissed, holding her still while he devoured her like his favorite sweet treat. Her heart thundered against her ribs and heat flooded her system. When he slid one finger, then two inside her, curling them to hit that magical spot, she screamed his name. She rocked against him, urging him on. Desire, hot and slick, surged through her. Tremors pulsated through her as he continued his assault until she climaxed in wave after wave of shimmering pleasure.

Once she'd stilled, he kissed his way up her slick, sweaty skin to press a kiss against her lips. She wrapped her arms around his neck again, so she wouldn't slide to the floor in a boneless heap.

"Take me to bed," she whispered against his mouth.

He caught one hand and led her to the suite's bedroom. They fell onto the bed together and she started laughing.

"Now I'm funny?" His brows drew together.

She giggled and pointed at him. "Well, I've got no bottoms and you've got no shirt and you have to admit it's kind of funny."

He glanced down and flashed his wicked grin. "Easy to fix. You lose your shirt and I'll get rid of these." He shifted onto his back and pulled off his shorts.

Toby might not be the tallest guy, but his long thick cock was a sight to behold. She licked her lips. "My turn."

In a quick move, she pushed him onto his back and straddled him. He groaned when she pressed her center along his length. "Fuck Grace."

"Shh, just lay back and enjoy." Just like she was going to enjoy tasting him.

She shifted back and dropped her head to nibble along his neck and her lips curved upward when goosebumps rose along his skin. Power filled her, loving how good it felt to give him pleasure. To feel him tremble under her kisses and caresses, the way he made her shake.

She skimmed her lips along his chest, pausing to lightly scrape her teeth along his small flat nipples. When she continued along the carved ridge of his abs, she savored the scent of soap and sweat and male––mouthwatering.

His breath was erratic now, the only sound filling the room. She kissed along the deep V-muscles and wrapped her fingers around him, lowered her head, and licked him from base to tip.

His back bowed up off the bed. "Grace."

She looked up at him. "I want you to watch." Serving him back his words.

She took her time, teasing and tasting, savoring him. Enjoying the velvety softness of his skin stretched tight over his hot hard cock.

"Grace, I'm not going to last. Please come here." His fingers tightened in her hair.

Taking her time, she kissed her way up his sweat-slickened body until she reached his mouth. He thrust his fingers into her hair and tugged her down to meet his eager kiss. His talented tongue danced and stroked against hers.

"That was incredible," he murmured without lifting his lips from hers.

She lifted her head and met his gaze in the dim light. "You're incredible. I want you inside me. Please tell me you have protection."

He searched her eyes, his wild and hot. "Are you sure?"

"Never been more sure of anything in my life." Nerves fluttered down her spine.

He shifted her to the side. "Don't move. I'll be right back."

Oh no, there wasn't anywhere else she'd rather be. She rolled onto her back and propped herself on the fluffy white mountain of pillows. Her skin was tingling, her heart was racing, and she wanted Toby McAvoy more than any man she'd ever met.

He strode into the room, all rippling muscles and wild hair. He reached the edge of the bed, waved the foil packet, and grinned. "Success."

"Thank god." She reached for the condom. "I want you."

His jaw tightened and his eyes darkened as he ripped open the packet and rolled on the condom. "I'm all yours."

Her heart took a long slow dive in her chest. He joined her, bracing his forearms on either side of her head. Anticipation shimmered through her. He lowered himself between her legs and without breaking her gaze, he entered her slowly, giving her time to adjust to his size.

A raw moan escaped her at the sensation of fullness, of connection. His eyes were hot, and he caressed her cheek with one hand before slanting his mouth against hers in a deep wild kiss.

"You feel incredible," he lifted his head, his voice rough and raw.

She raked her fingernails down the slick skin of his back. "You." She wrapped her legs around his hips, signaling she was ready for more.

He growled low in his throat and began to move in long, slow strokes. They found a rhythm, like this wasn't their first time. He never stopped kissing her, deep and dreamy, until tremors began to build inside her again. No sound existed except for their bodies' movement, the slick sweat on their skin, and their shared breath. He reached down to where they were connected and used his magic fingers until another shimmering climax blazed through her and she came apart with his name on her lips.

"Grace." He grasped her hips once again, holding her in place. He stroked two, three, four more times and followed her over the edge.

He dropped his head against her neck, his breath coming in harsh pants. She reached up and ran her hands through his messy hair. Oh my god.

He turned his head and pressed his lips against her throat. "Stay right here, I'll be right back."

Like she could move. He withdrew and strode to the bathroom to take care of the condom. But she could enjoy the view of his long lean muscles as they gleamed under the lights. Damn, he was hot. She stretched like a cat, savoring the dreamy satisfaction filling her, and her eyes drifted shut.

He joined her on the bed and pressed a tender kiss on her mouth. "You look pleased with yourself."

She opened her eyes and her lips curved upward. "Oh, I'm pleased with you."

He grinned. "Why, thank you. I'm pleased with both of us, but I'm wiped out."

"Me, too." Labyrinth all day and the marathon with Toby had definitely left her exhausted.

He pulled her back to his front, wrapped his arms around her, resting a possessive hand on her belly. "Sweet dreams."

She drifted off to sleep with a smile on her face and warmth in her heart.

$\sim$

GRACE RETURNED from the bathroom and paused to admire the picture Toby created. He lounged against the pillows; the white sheet draped around his hips. His bare chest and carved abs glistened in the early morning light.

His mouth curved up into a wicked grin, his green eyes gleamed, and he patted the sheets next to him. "Come here, beautiful. We have a few hours before we need to get up."

Nerves danced along her skin and her pulse thrummed in her throat. Sex with Toby had been incredible, but she'd woken up in the middle of the night and with each passing moment, grew more overwhelmed.

Time to have an adult conversation about the final round of the competition. Time to face the reality of their current situation. So why did she feel like running back to her room and burying her head under the pillows?

She crossed the room but hesitated, nibbling on her lip. "Toby, I--"

"Grace, I think we should make a plan for today. And for California. Don't be scared, I already bit you when you asked nicely." He winked.

Heat flooded her cheeks, and she tugged the towel she'd wrapped around her a little tighter. How she could feel shy after hours in his bed was a mystery. But the reality of their situation was flooding in. She perched on the edge of the bed, just out of reach. Safer that way.

She clasped her hands together in her lap. "What now?"

He tilted his head. "Well, if we didn't win the labyrinth, we won't be in the finals, and don't need to do anything. If we did win and compete against each other for the money, then we need to figure out how we play it."

Bile rose in her throat--how had she been so irresponsible and forgotten the reason she was here? Everything that was at stake?

"Grace?" His russet brows drew together.

She pressed her hands against her churning belly. "If I don't win, I'll have to close my non-profit. This is my last ditch effort, otherwise I'll lose everything. I can't even think about anything else."

If she didn't win the money, she'd have to shut the doors to her rescue and then what? Animals would suffer and she wouldn't have a career. Again.

He hissed out a breath. "I have people counting on me, too. You're not the only one with a lot to lose. But if we don't make it to the finals tomorrow, the money is a moot point."

"Well, what if we do? How are supposed to compete against each other now?" She dug her fingernails into her palms.

"Look, we can keep the competition and us separate, right? In front of the cameras, we play the game. I don't think either of us expected this to happen." He waved a hand between them.

She blew out an exhale. "This? What is this? We hooked up and talked about possibly seeing each other in California. What if this is all just the excitement of a holiday romance? We don't even live in the same town."

When up until a few days ago, she'd assumed he'd never be more than her rival?

His jaw tightened, he shifted back against the pillows and pulled the sheet up higher. "Hey, you were just as into this as I was. I like you and I thought you and I had a special connection. Outside of the cameras. You know, in real life. But maybe that was my mistake."

Had. Had a special connection. Already in the past tense. Her heart lurched. "We do have a connection and I do like you, but I can't even think about California until after the finals. I'm sorry. Maybe the smart thing to do is for me to go back to my room. And tomorrow we treat the competition as if nothing happened." *Even though I'm falling for you.*

"Like nothing happened?" His eyes cooled and his voice was dangerously quiet.

She pushed her tangled hair away from her face. "You're the one who said we should separate the personal and the professional. I'm just trying to do that. You know the producers probably have the footage of us kissing and will play up the romance angle hard.

"Both of us deserve to win but only one of us can. Both of us need to focus 100% on the game and not each other. Especially in front of the cameras." *And if I don't win, my focus at home will be picking up the pieces, not romance.*

"I guess I forgot you're an actress. You're making your point loud and clear. It's fine. And maybe it's better if you go back to your room. Good luck." He rose, wrapped the sheet around his hips, and strode to the bathroom, closing it with a decisive click.

She squeezed her eyes closed and forced herself to gather up her clothes, which were strewn all over the room. Her legs trembled and she blinked furiously against the tears threatening to spill onto her cheeks. No way would she cry. She'd chosen to step back from him. She was doing the smart thing.

She had to keep her priorities straight––when she made decisions based on emotion, she lost. And at the end of the day, she had to win this show. Cramming her feelings for Toby in the vault was the smart thing to do.

So why did she feel like she'd just ruined the most real connection she'd ever had?

CHAPTER 15

*G*race smoothed down the fabric of her silky white jumpsuit and focused on breathing slow and steady. Her hair hung in shiny waves around her shoulders. Despite slathering on sunscreen, her olive skin had darkened a few shades, and a couple freckles had popped out along her nose. The make-up artist slicked on a coat of killer red lipstick and left the rest of her face bare.

"You look glamorous and camera-ready. You happy with the look?" Keri, the stylist, asked.

She couldn't care less about how she looked right now but it was time to smile for the cameras. "It feels nice to be pampered and not be a sweaty, dirty mess like I've been for most of the week, so thank you."

After the way she'd crept out of Toby's room at dawn, she was a jumble of emotions. Flashbacks from the labyrinth and the most incredible night of her life flooded through her. Maybe she should have handled things differently. She hadn't meant to hurt his feelings, but she'd only spoken the truth. But now it was show time.

When she reached the courtyard, her expression was

composed. Toby stood at the far end of the group. When he saw her, his jaw tightened, and he turned away. She bit the inside of her cheek. Nothing she could do about it now.

Frances, dressed in a Stevie Nicks-style flowing dress and floppy hat, lifted the microphone from her customary spot on the stage. "Good morning, everyone, it's time to begin. Only three teams completed the labyrinth within the time limit. Two teams had to be located and escorted through the gates. It wasn't an easy challenge so bravo to all of you for your endurance and hard work."

Grace pressed both hands against her belly and looked around, trying to determine who else had finished. The only partners standing together were Isabella and Isaac and they were holding hands. Huh, maybe the producers' not-so-subtle matchmaking had brought those two back together. But now was the biggest moment of the competition so she directed her attention to the stage.

"The third and final round will reveal how much you learned about and from your assigned partner. It's a test of emotional intelligence and will assist me in choosing the final winner." Frances picked up a gilt-edged cream envelope and slid out a card. "The three teams who finished were Team #4, Kimmelle and Melissa, Team #1, Toby and Grace, and Team #2, Weston and Karina. Each one of you came in at under twelve hours, which is excellent.

"But exiting the labyrinth first is the winning requirement. The team competing for the one million dollars today will be Toby and Grace. Congratulations on finishing first in nine hours and twenty-two minutes. Let's put our hands together for a job well done."

Applause filled the courtyard. Although happiness bloomed inside her--she hadn't been eliminated--it was tempered with bittersweet. Winning the game and saving her charity was her reason for being here, so she should be over-joyed. But she struggled to keep her smile in place.

This morning, all she could think of was how she may have jeopardized everything by allowing her burgeoning feelings for Toby to take over. And in the process, she'd been harsher with him than she'd intended.

"Toby and Grace, please come join me on the stage."

She swallowed her nerves and crossed the space with Toby, who wore his customary nonchalant smile. He didn't meet her eyes. Maybe he was just playing it cool for the cameras and the ultimate prize.

Once they stood next to Frances, she continued, "This final round is an homage to one of my favorite game shows from the 1970s, which aired before any of you were born. It's a true test to see how well Toby and Grace bonded during their time working together.

"This finale is modeled after The Newlywed Game. I will ask questions and Toby and Grace will write down answers separately. Then, we'll see how many they guess correctly about the other.

"The true test will come down to one final question, but we'll save that for the game. Surprises and all that. Let's move into the ballroom." Frances smiled.

Grace pressed one hand to her belly——now a mass of knots. The producers hadn't been kidding when they claimed this show was like no other. She turned and trooped into a high-ceilinged room, complete with crystal chande-liers and enormous rectangular windows. Rays of sunshine streamed into the space, in stark contrast to the huge cameras and artificial lighting.

Lights, camera, action.

She squared her shoulders and climbed the few stairs to the competition stage that looked like they'd stepped into the 1970s, complete with multicolored curtains, two white plastic seats, and a low table which held posterboard and Sharpies.

She peeked at Toby, but he continued to avoid her gaze. Great. If she could focus during this game, she'd apologize and deal with all the unfamiliar feelings later. If he would even speak with her. Nothing to do now but play the game. And win.

Frances acted as the game show host, and they plowed through some basic questions, like hometowns, pets' names, and who chose the most correct turns in the labyrinth. At the end of the ten questions, they were tied.

"Well, we're at the final question, which will decide who will be walking away with one million dollars for their charity. If you remain tied, there will be an extra question at the end to determine the winner if necessary."

Frances paused and looked at the camera, her crimson lips pursed, her eyes wide. "Will it be Grace for her animal rescue Golden Years Pet Sanctuary or Toby, for Alpine Adaptive Athlete Foundation? Are you two ready?"

Grace gripped her pen so tightly, it was a miracle the ink hadn't exploded everywhere. Her heart knocked against her ribcage and a fine sheen of sweat pasted her clothes to her skin.

"Here is the question. Please respond how you think the other person would answer. Grace, if Toby won the prize do you think he would keep all the money, offer to split the money with you, or give you the entire prize because he believes you deserve it more? And Toby, same question about Grace, if it was an option."

"But who wins? Isn't there just one prize?" Isabella shouted from the audience.

Frances held up one finger and winked at the camera. "There may be a twist but please hold your commentary until the finalists respond."

Grace smoothed a strand of hair behind her ear. *What?* A twist? What did that even mean? And how would they even determine the winner now? This made no sense at all. But what choice did she have?

Think, she needed to think.

From what Toby had shared with her, he still harbored guilt over his friend's injury and had walked away from his pro-athlete career in his prime. Like her, he'd dedicated the last several years to helping people. He was a generous, giving person and deserved to win. But they both did. So what would he write down?

Her gut told her he wouldn't take all the money. Unlike her mother and ex-best friend, he wasn't ruthless and out only for himself. He wasn't a Hollywood guy. Maybe $500k wouldn't be enough for either of their non-profits, but it would be a temporary solution. And it had to be enough.

He'd do the fair thing and split it between them. Wouldn't he? Or maybe he would have before she'd messed things up this morning. *Here goes nothing.* She nibbled on her lower lip and wrote down her response.

Toby had already capped his pen and set it on the table. He turned and caught her gaze, his green eyes warm now, his lips curved into a crooked smile. Hope flickered through her––maybe they'd both walk away partial winners. And maybe there was a chance for something more in California.

"Grace, please hold up your card," Frances said.

She held up her response and gasps erupted around the room. Toby sucked in a sharp inhale and when she glanced at him, he'd squeezed his eyes closed. Her heart dropped.

"How generous of you, Grace. Now let's see if Toby is on the same page." Frances nodded and her lips curved upward.

Toby lifted his card and shocked cries came from the audience. Grace leaned forward and read his response.

"Give the entire prize away."

Her breath hitched. "Toby, why would you do that?"

He angled toward her, his expression bleak. "You're one of the most caring, giving people I've ever met. You deserve to win the prize. And I figured you would think the same thing about me, and we would have the same answer."

Her belly twisted into knots. She opened her mouth to respond but nothing came out. She cleared her throat and tried again.

"Nobody has ever helped me like that. I know how much you need the money, too. But I never expected you to give it all away or offer it to me. I figured you'd say split it, too, so we'd both win."

He looked down and massaged the back of his neck.

Grace whirled toward Frances. "This doesn't make any sense. Now who wins? And what if we had both answered the same thing? What is going on?"

Frances grinned like the Cheshire cat and clapped her hands together. "You're correct. It doesn't make any sense, but this is *my* game and I get to make the rules. I declare you both winners.

"Connection is important and being able to work with different personalities during challenges is vital. Many a great organization has fallen apart because of personal issues between the people. Your partnerships were not chosen at random."

Frances paused and gazed around the room, letting that nugget sink in. Because obviously they'd put Toby and her together after observing their chemistry. And they had been perfect partners, in every sense of the word. Had she ruined any chance of them exploring a relationship once the show ended?

"If one of you had answered keep all the money for yourself, the other would have won. But since you both exhibited care and compassion for the other person, at the expense of yourself, you demonstrated the characteristic I want in my winners--compassion and generosity of spirit. So you will each take home one million dollars."

For a moment, the room fell silent. Then shouts and applause echoed off the high ceiling.

They'd both won? Excitement raced through her--Golden Years Pet Sanctuary could not only continue, but she could expand and save even more animals than she'd dreamed possible. And Toby's foundation was secure. It was surreal.

She jumped up from her seat and pressed her hands to her heart. "Frances, I don't know how I'll ever be able to thank you."

"Continuing your good work is thanks enough. You can share photos of the sweet animals with their new families."

Toby spoke from beside her. "Thank you so much for your generosity. This week has been quite the experience. I'm excited to keep my foundation going and continue working with adaptive athletes."

"You earned it with your excellent teamwork. I didn't think any of you would navigate my labyrinth so quickly. Impressive. Now, I will need you both to head over to the interview booth to answer some more questions. The rest of the contestants will also each answer some final questions, so please remain in the courtyard. You have the afternoon free and our final celebration dinner this evening. Your plane will leave tomorrow. Thank you, everyone."

She turned to Toby, but he was already heading off stage with Betsy.

Her shoulders slumped. Yes, she'd won one million dollars, but had she blown any chance with Toby?

CHAPTER 16

Interview Booth: Winner's Circle

TOBY SETTLED into the cramped space that felt more like a police interrogation room than an interview booth. Not that he'd been arrested before, but he'd seen them on television. No matter how many "conversations" he'd had with the camera screen, it was impossible to act natural. Although after the one-two punch of Grace bailing early this morning and them choosing different responses, he'd put on his poker face and wasn't going to let it slip.

"Congratulations Toby," a disembodied voice said from the speakers across from him. "How do you feel?"

Loaded question, that one. He gave a thumbs up. "Awesome. I'm super stoked to head back to California knowing that I can expand on my mission to help injured athletes get a second chance to practice the sports they love."

"That's great. Are they all snowboarders like you?"

He shook his head. "Snowboarders, skiers, alpine hikers.

What they have in common is that their injuries prevent them from doing what they did before. But now, there are ways for them to get back on the mountain with a variety of adaptive skis and more. They can experience the freedom of the wind on their faces as they speed down the slopes." Fresh energy filled him. He'd done it.

"Amazing. And a wonderful cause. But you were willing to give it all to Grace. Tell us why?"

He sucked in a sharp inhale. Yeah, they'd lulled him into a sense of security before digging into what they really cared about. *Jerks.*

He dragged his hand through his hair, taking a moment so he could answer calmly. "I think I made it pretty clear when I presented my answer. She'd have to close her charity if she lost, and I have more resources––not that I don't need this money––but she's deserving." *And I fell for her.*

"So it has nothing to do with that passionate kiss outside the labyrinth's center tower?"

His nostrils flared and he gritted his teeth. "Nothing at all."

"Grace was an award-winning actress. Do you think she kissed you as a game strategy? Pretending interest for the cameras? Because you gave her everything and she kept half, right?"

"Grace hasn't been on television in years. We were just excited when we finished the labyrinth, that's all. And, you know, she's easy on the eyes." *Don't let them stir up a reaction.*

"Okay, sure. Congrats again, Toby."

The camera light went dark. He tore off his mic and stalked out of the room. Man, was he that obvious? He didn't believe Grace had played him for the show but judging by this morning, she didn't feel the same as he did.

And her response didn't even surprise him that much now that he considered it. Nobody had sacrificed for her before so why would she anticipate he would? Hell, he understood why she'd run away this morning, too.

But he had to protect himself. He always fell for the wrong woman and ended up getting screwed over. No matter how much he liked her, how intense their chemistry was, how easily he could see falling--truly falling--for Grace, she wasn't on the same page.

Time to head back to his bungalow and prepare to play it cool until they flew home tomorrow. Because that would be so simple.

∼

"CONGRATULATIONS, Grace. Way to play the game and walk away with the money. What's the first thing you'll do when you get back to California?" The monotone voice blared through the speaker.

Play the game for a little longer. She flashed a wide smile. "Thank you. When I get home, the first thing I'll do is cuddle with my cat Luna and the second will be to set up a meeting with my Board to discuss the best way to use the funds for the sanctuary."

"That's great. Such a wonderful cause saving animals. Maybe I'll have to come in and adopt one myself."

And they were buttering her up for the kill. Grace managed not to roll her eyes. "Absolutely."

"Now tell us your first thought when Toby offered to give up one million dollars and hand it to you. Why would he do that?"

There it was. She inhaled a steadying breath and stared directly into the camera. "I was shocked, to tell you the truth. You probably saw that."

"But he had to have believed you'd answer the same way. Why would he think you'd give up the money?"

What part of "shocked" didn't register? They were angling for something specific from her. Something juicy. No way would she give it to them. "I'm really not sure. He's a generous guy." She shrugged a shoulder.

"So you didn't make any promises to each other after that kiss in the labyrinth? A pact?"

Her spine stiffened but she kept her face neutral. "A pact? Not sure for what since we didn't know what the finale would be nor if we'd win the labyrinth. And no promises." Of course the editors would have a field day with their kiss. It would probably end up on the cover of *People* magazine.

"Okay, well, congratulations again, Grace. Way to win the game." And the camera clicked off.

She rose from the uncomfortable wooden chair and exited the tiny room. Thank god this was the last time she had to deal with this interview booth.

Right now, she needed to be alone and process Toby's choice and how they'd both won the prize money for their charities. She hurried down the stone path toward her bungalow. Would he hear her out now that the competition was over?

CHAPTER 17

"Toby, wait up," Grace called from the edge of the clearing.

He stopped a few feet from the Jeep. Took a steadying breath.

She reached him and brushed one soft hand along his arm. "Can we please talk?"

He turned and his breath lodged in his throat. Damn, she was so fucking beautiful, especially now that he knew her. Or thought he knew her. Her resilience, her compassionate heart, her clever brain.

"Toby?" She tilted her head, her crystal blue eyes wide, her dark hair falling in soft waves around her face.

"I don't know that we've got much to talk about." He needed space to lick his wounds and process what had happened, not to spend more time with her.

She took a deep breath and stepped closer. "I think we do. I want to talk about this morning and how terribly I handled that conversation. I want to talk about our choices on that final question. I want to talk about California. I want to talk about us."

He gazed down and rubbed the scruff on his jaw before looking at her. "You're ready to talk now you've won?"

She bit her plump lower lip. "I deserve that comment. But you obviously understand how much was at stake for me or you wouldn't have chosen to say you'd give me the money. Now that we don't have the show between us, can we talk about the real world? Please?"

His heart tightened. "I was going to drive up to Artemis's Temple. Want to come with me?"

"I do."

They climbed into the SUV, and he navigated along the winding roads, enjoying the salty ocean air, and the glimpses of cerulean water. Not to mention how good it felt to have Grace beside him. At least for now.

Who knew how their talk would go? He glanced over and she turned toward him with a bright smile. His fingers tightened on the steering wheel--she stole his breath.

Once they pulled into the small lot surrounded by low stone walls and fields of fiery flowers, he parked.

She rounded the front of the vehicle. "Want to head over to our bench?"

"Our bench?"

She waved a hand. "Okay, the bench."

"Sure." It was the spot where they'd kissed for the first time. So, yeah, maybe it was their bench.

The gravel crunched beneath their feet as they crossed to the ancient stone temple. The sun shone bright in the afternoon sky. Unfamiliar nerves skittered down his spine.

When she sat down, he joined her, but on the far end of the bench. Despite the distance, the chemistry hummed in the air between them. No surprise--their physical attraction wasn't their issue. Everything else was. And he wasn't a person used to talking about his feelings. So he waited.

She clasped her slender hands together and turned to

him. "Okay, I'm terrible at talking about emotions. But I want to apologize. I freaked out this morning about everything. I didn't expect to fall," She paused and cleared her throat. "I mean, I didn't expect to like you so much. And I didn't expect I wouldn't be able to control myself.

"I've been on my own for what seems like forever, and it takes me a long time to allow people close. So the fact I couldn't keep my hands off you and risked the future of my non-profit terrified me."

A sense of lightness filled him, and his lips twitched. "So you're letting me in close and you can't keep your hands off me? I'm irresistible?"

"Oh, you think that's funny? It's not like you can keep your hands off me either." Her dark brows winged up.

"I never pretended I could. Hell, I couldn't get away from you fast enough in the tug-o-war."

She smirked. "You did make a scene. I was so mad at you."

"I did what I had to do for the team. We would have lost if I hadn't."

Her expression grew serious, her eyes gleaming with genuine emotion. "I can't believe you offered to give me all the money."

He shrugged. "Well, technically, Frances told us to answer how we thought the other person would answer. I figured you were such a softie with your three-legged cat and animal sanctuary that you'd say the same thing. But I know Golden Years is everything to you. So..."

She skimmed her fingers along his jaw. "I think you're the softie, Fox."

He caught her hand and pressed a kiss to her cool palm. "For you. Look, this show, meeting you––it's been a lot. All I know is I like you. I like you a lot. I'd like to see you when we get back to California. I want to take you on a proper date. Have sleepovers."

She laughed. "Sleepovers?"

He tugged her closer and clasped her face in his hands. "Yeah, sleepovers. Because you left me way before the alarm went off this morning. And since we don't live in the same town, I think it would be the smart strategy."

"Oh, we're talking about strategy again?" Her pupils flared.

He closed the distance between them and captured her tempting mouth. Her lips parted on a moan, and she deepened the kiss, winding her arms around his neck. Her tongue danced and tangled with his, her sweet breath and delicious taste sending heat curling down his spine.

After a while, he lifted his head. Artemis's Temple probably wasn't the best place for them right now. The back seat of the Jeep or his bungalow was where they needed to go. Pronto.

"How about we head back? We've got the rest of the day free, right? I've got this great little pool on my patio." He winked.

Her eyelids were heavy, and her lips swollen from his kisses. Damn, she was the sexiest woman he'd ever met. "So this means you've forgiven me?"

"As long as you tell me you'll see me when we get back."

She grinned. "I like you a lot. And I definitely want to see you when we get home. I'd love to see where this goes. I'm down in Redondo Beach and you're in Leucadia, so we're less than two hours apart. I think we can make it work."

Elation surged through him. "Like I said earlier, it will be a piece of cake."

She rose and reached for his hand. "I don't know if it's been a piece of cake but meeting you has made all of this much sweeter."

They sauntered back to the Jeep and toward the future.

EPILOGUE

*S**even Months Later:*
Leucadia, California

"Can I have everyone's attention, please?" Grace tapped her champagne flute against Toby's. The bright shiny lobby of Golden Years Pet Sanctuary's new location was packed with people and animals. Between the barking, chattering, and laughter, nobody looked up. Even though she held a microphone.

Toby squeezed her waist with one strong hand. "Need me to whistle?"

She laughed and gazed into his gleaming green eyes. "Yeah, I don't think we'll get in a toast if you don't."

Toby placed two fingers in his mouth and blew. "Listen up, everyone." The piercing whistle got not just the two-legged creatures to look up, but also the four-legged ones.

"Thanks, babe." She smiled at him before addressing the crowd.

"I wanted to thank each and every one of you for being

here tonight. Earlier this year, I was afraid we would have to close my beloved sanctuary but thanks to Celebrity Charity Champions and the generosity of Frances Ellis, we were able to renovate this amazing property and start fresh here in North County San Diego."

Cheers and applause filled the high-ceilinged space.

Happiness sparkled through her. "Frances is here tonight and we're filming the party for a follow-up to the show. We've also got several lovely senior animals here tonight who are ready to live out their sunset years being spoiled rotten. Volunteers are walking dogs around the party, and you can also go to the cat house to meet our available kitties.

"Please enjoy the delicious food created by the incredible Melissa and chat up our other celebrities from the show who are here tonight. Adoption applications are on the back table if you meet your perfect new pet."

It warmed her heart to see all the contestants had shown up, even Clay. Isabella and Isaac waved from the back of the room. The show had brought them back together and they were planning a winter wedding. Toby's friend Josh sat at one of the picnic tables, chatting with Karina, who had flown in from Paris for the grand opening. Grant and Olivia, Toby's childhood best friends and "Musketeers" toasted with their champagne flutes.

Toby pulled Grace into his embrace. "I'm so proud of you."

She dropped her head onto his shoulder. "It never could have happened without you. I love you so much."

"I love you. too. And I'm so glad you love it down here and moved in with me." He clasped her jaw in his hand and pressed a long, sweet kiss on her lips.

Joy bubbled through her. "You know I was happy to finally escape L.A. No more cameras and microphones after tonight."

He stepped back and shoved his wild hair away from his face. "Oh, can I see the microphone for a minute? I wanted to announce one more thing."

"Did I forget something? I'm sorry, should I have talked about your foundation?" She placed the mic in his hand.

He didn't meet her eyes. "No, no. Frances and the film crew will be in Mammoth Mountain covering the adaptive mountain games."

He caught her hand and pulled her in close to his side. "Toby?"

"Hey everyone, I've got something to say. Thanks again for coming tonight. I want to thank Frances and everyone from Celebrity Charity Champions because that show changed my life. Changed our lives." He turned and gazed at her, his eyes gleaming with genuine emotion, with love.

Her heart took a slow rolling dive in her chest and her fingers tightened with his.

"I went to Greece to win money for my foundation and thought it would be simple. But then I met this incredible woman. She's not only beautiful on the outside, but she's funny, smart, compassionate, and has a freakishly deep knowledge of labyrinths."

People laughed and tapped their glasses, but the buzz of the crowd was fading away. Everything was fading away except for the sincerity in Toby's gaze. Her legs trembled and her pulse kicked up.

He dropped to one knee and whipped out a small velvet box. "Grace Steele, I love you and I want to spend the rest of my life showing you just how much. Will you marry me?"

Her breath whooshed out and she pressed her hands against her mouth.

He flipped open the lid, revealing a princess cut diamond set in a delicate platinum setting.

"Yes, Toby, yes. I love you so much." She extended her hand, and he slipped the ring on her finger. "It's perfect."

She admired the sparkling gem before tugging him to his feet and throwing her arms around him. Happiness sparkled through her. "Kiss me."

He flashed his crooked grin. "One more for the cameras?"

Why not? "One more for the cameras. On our terms."

He clasped her face in his hands and slanted his mouth across hers in a deep passionate kiss. She melted against him, savoring the feel of his hard body and delicious taste.

They stepped apart and raised the microphone once more. "Let's celebrate."

Hand in hand, they stepped off the stage and toward the rest of their lives.

Pacific Vista Ranch Series

Nobody Else But You

The Very Thought of You

For The Love of You

Wrapped Up with You

The Wonder of You

California Suits Series

Hotel King

Wine Country King

Monterey King

Holiday Queen

Palm Springs King

Beverly Hills King

True Stars Collide (related novella)

Romance in Laguna Beach Series

Second Chance in Laguna

At Last in Laguna

Sunset in Laguna

: ACKNOWLEDGMENTS

Readers have been asking about Toby ever since he appeared as one of the "Three Musketeers," alongside Grant and Olivia in *The Wonder of You*. When Grant and Olivia found their HEA, Toby started to feel like a third wheel. I hadn't planned on writing his story but this fun idea for a reality TV show/rivals to lovers story popped up! I hope you enjoyed reading it as much as I enjoyed writing it.

Thank you to all the readers who read my books! I love writing them and as long as you keep reading…I'll keep going! Thank you for allowing me to live my dream.

I want to thank my wonderful beta readers: Donna Simonetta, Joanna Kelly, my brother Robert, and Sara Martin —I couldn't do this without your helpful and insightful feedback! For the lovely author friends I've made along the way, with whom I share such a sense of camaraderie, thanks for being there: Christina Hovland, Serena Bell, Katie O'Sullivan, Krista Sandor, Charlotte O'Shay, Donna Simonetta and so many more.

To my wonderful editor, Lindsey Faber, thank you for your consistently excellent suggestions, keen insight, brilliant ideas, and the way you push me to make each story better. Thank you to Shasta Schafer for your skillful proofreading. Thank you Sarah Paige for the beautiful covers you create.

Last but not least, to Todd for being the best husband in the world. I love you. And, finally to my furry kids: Lola, Beau, Josie, and Daisy thanks for providing me daily laughs and all the cuddles.

ABOUT THE AUTHOR

Claire Marti is an award winning and *USA Today* Bestselling author of swoonworthy Contemporary Romance novels set in Southern California, including the California Suits series, Pacific Vista Ranch series, and the Romance in Laguna Beach series. She lives in San Diego with her husband, silly dog, and three clever cats.

Claire started writing stories as soon as she was old enough to pick up pencil and paper. After graduating from the University of Virginia with a BA in English Literature, Claire was sidetracked by other careers, including practicing law, selling software for legal publishers, and managing a non-profit animal rescue for a Hollywood actress.

Finally, Claire followed her heart and now focuses on two of her true passions: writing romance and teaching yoga.